Bang!

Amber awoke with a start at the loud noise and was suddenly struggling to breathe as Dex threw himself on top of her, his gaze darting around the room.

"What's going on?" she whispered, as she tried to extricate herself from beneath him, very aware that her nightshirt had ridden up to her belly and that Dex had apparently shed all of his clothes during the night except for his boxers.

He glanced down at her as if only just now seeing her, then rolled off her. "Are you okay?"

"I think so. What was that noise?"

"Gunshot."

She stared at him in shock. "Are you sure it wasn't thunder?" As if in response to her question, thunder boomed overhead and another incredible wave of rain began pouring in earnest.

"That sound came from inside the house."

ARRESTING DEVELOPMENTS

LENA DIAZ

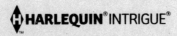

HARLEQUIN® INTRIGUE®

Thank you, Allison Lyons and Nalini Akolekar.

ISBN-13: 978-0-373-74935-5

Arresting Developments

Copyright © 2016 by Lena Diaz

This edition published by arrangement with Harlequin Books S.A.

For questions and comments about the quality of this book, please contact us at CustomerService@Harlequin.com.

Lena Diaz was born in Kentucky and has also lived in California, Louisiana and Florida, where she now resides with her husband and two children. Before becoming a romantic suspense author, she was a computer programmer. A former Romance Writers of America Golden Heart Award finalist, she has won a prestigious Daphne du Maurier Award for excellence in mystery and suspense. To get the latest news about Lena, please visit her website, lenadiaz.com.

Books by Lena Diaz

Marshland Justice

Missing in the Glades
Arresting Developments

Harlequin Intrigue

The Marshal's Witness
Explosive Attraction
Undercover Twin
Tennessee Takedown
The Bodyguard

Visit the Author Profile page at Harlequin.com for more titles.

CAST OF CHARACTERS

Dex Lassiter—This PI crashes his Cessna in the Everglades and right into the middle of a murder mystery. Temporarily deputized as Mystic Glades' only (and temporary) law enforcement officer, he soon wonders whether the woman at the center of the investigation is a murderess. Or a victim?

Amber Callahan—She hides in the Everglades to avoid a murder charge, and gives up her freedom to save the life of an airplane crash survivor. But after several dangerous developments, she must find out whether someone is trying to kill her, or the man she saved.

Freddie Callahan—Amber's whiskey-loving aunt is the owner and bartender of Callahan's Watering Hole in the quirky town of Mystic Glades. But her lack of support for her niece could be suspicion of Amber, or her own guilt. Who *really* killed Freddie's father?

Mitchell Fielding—Dex's business assistant. What's the real reason he travels to Mystic Glades? Does he want to help his boss, or destroy him?

Garreth Jackson—Lawyer for Dex's firm, Garreth steps in to help Amber with her legal troubles. But Dex soon learns there's more to his lawyer than he ever realized.

Buddy Johnson—Longtime resident of Mystic Glades and owner of Swamp Buggy Outfitters, Buddy knows more about Amber's grandfather's death than anyone realizes.

Derek Slater—Dex's longtime friend and wingman on many dates, has Derek tagged along on the trip to Mystic Glades to help Dex? Or does his friendly exterior harbor something far more sinister?

Chapter One

Dex looked out the cockpit window of his Cessna Corvalis at the vast wasteland of the Everglades racing below him at 190 knots. The monotony of sand-colored saw grass went on for miles, broken only by occasional muddy canals and vast islands of mangled cypress, their roots sticking out of the brackish water like giant knobby knees. If the Glades were anything like the marshes back home in Saint Augustine, he didn't know how anyone could stand the rotten-egg stink of rotting vegetation enough to want to visit for very long, let alone live there.

"I don't get it, Jake." He held his cell phone to his ear while he looked out the windows. "You worked your butt off to convince me to front the money to create Lassiter and Young Private Investigations. But just a few months after leaving everyone you know—including me—and setting up shop in Naples,

you're ready to close the doors. For what—
this swamp full of smelly plants and more alligators per capita than people? Can't you get
Faye to move instead of *you* moving to Mystic Glades?"

He maneuvered the stick and dipped the
wing, veering from his flight plan for a bird's-
eye view of the town that had been at the center of their recent investigation but was now
going to be his friend's new home. *Unless Dex
could talk him out of it.*

"Hold it," Jake said. "What do you mean
'this' swamp? Aren't you still in north Florida?"

"I was. But then you called last week to tell
me that you and the former target of our first
and only case were an item and that you were
quitting. I left my billion-dollar enterprise on
the brink of ruin with people I barely trust so
I could talk you out of this foolishness."

Jake snorted. "Don't give me that. Lassiter
Enterprises runs so smoothly no one will
even notice that you're gone. More than likely,
you're using me as an excuse to hide from the
latest girlfriend you dumped. Who is it this
time? That intellectual property rights attorney
you introduced me to last Christmas? Didn't
you date her for several months? I thought you

two were getting serious. Veronica something-or-other?"

"You wound me deeply to imply that I would use our friendship as an excuse to avoid my commitment issues."

"Uh-huh. What's the name of the woman you're running from this time?"

"Mallory. I think she wants to kill me."

"They usually do. Dex? *Exactly* where are you?"

He tapped the touch screen of the GPS navigation system. "Good question. My state-of-the-art airplane isn't acting so state-of-the-art right now. It's blinking like a caution light on steroids." The screen went dark. "What the…?" He rapped the glass with his fist.

"Tell me you aren't flying over Mystic Glades," Jake said.

Dex looked out the side window. "As a matter of fact, I think I am. And it doesn't look any better from up here than I thought it would. I count fifteen, maybe twenty ramshackle wooden buildings down one long dirt road. Looks like something out of the Old West, or a ghost town, or both. Where are the houses? Where are the cars? Heck, where's the *town*? Is that all there is?"

"It's bigger than it looks. There are side roads hidden under the tree canopies. It's fairly spread out. And most of the townspeople use canoes or ATVs to get around more than they use cars. But I'm pretty sure I've told you most of that already. Do you even remember our last call? The one where I said I was *getting married*?"

"I remember *that* part. It was right before you said 'I quit.'" He pressed the stick, nosing the plane lower while pulling up on the throttle to reduce air speed for another circle. "This place is in the middle of *no*where—as in *no* bars, *no* nightclubs, probably *no* satellite service. How are you going to keep up with football season out here? I-75 or Alligator Alley or whatever the locals call it is the closest thing resembling civilization, but that's miles away. Tell me what it is about this place that you find so appealing, 'cause I'm sure not seeing it."

"I didn't catch everything you said. The cell service near Mystic Glades is unpredictable at best. But I *can* tell you the town has a way of growing on you. About me getting married— I may have…"

The phone went silent. Dex pulled it back to look at it. The call still showed active. He put the phone back to his ear. "Jake?"

"Still here. Can you hear me?"

"I can now. Hang on a sec." He thumped the instrument panel again, but it remained dark, useless. Thankfully, it was a clear summer day with good visibility. But he was going to raise hell with the manufacturer when he got home. The plane was just a few months out of its shiny new wrapping and still had that new-plane smell. It shouldn't have had *any* issues, let alone a full instrumentation meltdown. He shook his head in disgust. Maybe he should get into the airplane manufacturing business instead of high finance and investing in other people's ventures. He could teach those yahoos a thing or two about quality standards.

"Dex?"

"Yeah. You said something about getting engaged?"

"Uh, about that. We decided on a very short engagement. We're already married."

Dex noisily tapped the side of the phone. "This thing must be messing up again because it sounded like you said you already got hitched. Without inviting me to the ceremony. Which means you can kiss the shamelessly extravagant gift I would have gotten you goodbye. Wait…*when* did you get married?"

"That's what I'm trying to tell you. We did the deed yesterday. We're in the Bahamas for the next two weeks. Freddie—Faye's friend, the one who owns Callahan's Watering Hole— gave us the trip as a wedding present."

Dex shook his head and sent the plane into a turn, heading in what he believed was a southwesterly direction toward Naples Municipal Airport. He'd rather head straight home to Saint Augustine, but he couldn't risk flying that far with a dead instrument panel. "Looks like this was a wasted trip."

"Sorry, man. I had no idea you'd fly out there without telling me first."

"Honestly, I didn't, either. But when I complained about you quitting our little business experiment, my assistant encouraged me to surprise you. He insisted it would be good for me to get away. And I figured I might be able to talk you out of a big mistake. Guess I should have come sooner."

"Marrying Faye *wasn't* a mistake," Jake bit out, sounding aggravated.

"Okay, okay. Sorry. I will graciously admit defeat. I guess I have to welcome Faye into the family now. Maybe I'll even buy you two a present after all."

"Gee, thanks."

"Hey, what can I say? I'm a softie."

"When we get back, I'll call you and we'll decide what to do about the company. You could always try to make a go of it without me. Just drop 'Young' from the name."

"Without my former-police-detective partner there'd be no point. Who'd want to hire an ex-navy pilot turned financier to hunt down a cheating husband or find a missing person?"

"I couldn't have solved Faye's case without your help. You're not too shabby as an amateur sleuth."

"Yeah. I can search the internet and make phone calls with the best of them."

"Actually, most of the time that's exactly what detectives do—research and interview witnesses." A woman's voice sounded in the background. Jake murmured something to her, then cleared his throat. "I've, ah, got to go."

"Wait. Jake?"

"Yeah?"

"All kidding aside. Are you sure about this? About Faye? You haven't known her very long, and half that time you were taking turns pointing guns at each other. I just… I want to know that you're going to be okay."

"Are you getting sentimental on me, Dex?"

"I don't even know what that word means."

Jake laughed. "Well, you don't have to worry. I may not have planned this, but Faye's the best thing that ever happened to me. I love her. She's my whole world."

The certainty in his friend's voice went a long way toward reassuring Dex. Maybe Faye was what Jake needed to heal him from the mistakes of his past. God knows he'd had his share of tragedy and was long overdue for some happiness.

"Then I look forward to meeting her. Enjoy your honeymoon." The call cut out as Jake was saying goodbye. Dex shook his head again and put the phone away as he tried to judge his altitude. Lower than he was comfortable with. He was about to edge the nose up to climb higher when he noticed a young woman in a canoe.

Her dark brown hair hung in waves to the middle of her back. Even from the cockpit he could see the long, shapely tanned legs that paired nicely with a curvy body wearing only a skimpy yellow tank top and khaki shorts. He whistled low in admiration. She looked better than anything he'd seen in months. He just wished he could make out the details of her face to see if it matched the rest of the sexy package.

On impulse, he waved at her, but she didn't wave back. She might not have seen him waving, but more likely she probably thought he was an idiot. He couldn't blame her for that. He was about to increase air speed when a thick mist seemed to come from out of nowhere and wrapped around the plane like a shroud. He tapped the instrument panel again, hoping he could at least get an altimeter reading. Nothing. He was flying blind.

A scraping noise sounded against the bottom of the plane. He cursed and put it into a climb. The mist suddenly cleared. An enormous cypress tree stood dead ahead, its moss-covered branches reaching out like giant claws.

He banked hard left while throttling up. The branches made a sickening scraping noise against the underbelly of his Cessna, but she did her job, clearing the deadly tree. He laughed with relief and wiped a bead of sweat from his brow. That was close—too close.

A dull thump sounded from the engine. An alarming shudder ran through the fuselage, making the springs in his seat rattle. Instead of the familiar, reassuring dull roar of the twin turbocharged power plant, all he heard now was the sound of air rushing past the windows. He watched in stunned disbelief as the single propeller began to slow.

The engine had just died.

He immediately tried a restart with no luck. At such a low altitude there wasn't much room to recover. The controls were sluggish. He fought to keep the plane on an even keel and catch some lift beneath the wings while continuing the restart attempt. But it was a losing battle with the engine refusing to catch.

He flipped the button on his headset to make the one call he'd hoped never to have to make, and never *had* made in all his years of flying fighter jets in the navy.

"Mayday, Mayday, Mayday. Naples Municipal, this is Bravo Two Seven One Charlie Baker, a Cessna TTX with total engine failure attempting a forced landing in the Everglades. Last known location approximately two nautical miles southeast of Mystic Glades. Mayday, Mayday, Mayday."

No answer. Not even static.

AMBER FOUGHT DOWN her panic and paddled her canoe toward shore. The pilot in that fancy little green-and-white plane had waved at her. But that didn't necessarily mean that he'd recognized her. Maybe he was the friendly type. It wasn't like there was an airport in Mystic Glades, so he was probably just a stranger passing overhead. She'd hidden out here for over two years without anyone finding her. There was no reason to fear the worst now.

Tell that to her shaking hands.

She reached the shore and realized she could no longer hear the plane's engine. The noise had stopped suddenly instead of fading away. A sickening feeling shot through her stomach. She hopped out of the canoe and ran around a clump of trees to look up at the sky in the direction where the plane had gone. It was a small spec now, probably more than a mile away. As she watched, the wings dipped back and forth and the plane dropped alarmingly low. Then it lifted, as if it were gliding and had caught a rush of air, before tilting crazily and disappearing behind a line of trees.

She clenched her hands together, waiting for the plane to rise above the trees again. *Come on, come on.* A full minute passed. Nothing. No plane. No sounds but the usual insects and frogs that created a constant low buzz that rarely ever stopped. He couldn't have crashed. There would have been smoke, wouldn't there? But if he hadn't crashed, she'd have seen the plane again.

Maybe he was one of the drug runners who used the Everglades as their own private highway to ferry their poison from city to city. But usually they used boats to get through the canals. And the plane she'd seen couldn't land on the water. It was sleek and expensive looking, like a minijet with a propeller—without a pontoon in sight.

She started forward, then stopped. *No. Don't try to help him.* People who can afford planes like that don't just disappear. Someone will notice that he's missing. They'll send a search party. At the most, he'll be out here a couple of hours while they figure out how to reach the crash site.

If he'd even survived the crash.

Outsiders would need guides through the swamp. Guides meant hiring locals, most likely from Mystic Glades, which meant soon the place would be crawling with people who *would* recognize her.

She ran to the canoe. Grasping the sides, she put one foot on the bottom, ready to shove off with the other.

What if he survived the crash? What if he's hurt? What if he's hurt so badly that he needs immediate care?

She *couldn't* help him. That wasn't something she did anymore. She'd learned that lesson the most painful way possible. A familiar stab of grief and guilt threatened to overwhelm her. But she ruthlessly locked those useless emotions away.

Okay, assume he's not hurt. He can find his own way to Mystic Glades. But he could just as easily wander into the swamp and get lost. He could stumble into a nest of alligators or step on a snake. The Glades might be beautiful but they were dangerous, teeming with wildlife, emphasis on *wild*. Only those who understood its dangers—and respected them—could avoid them and thrive out here.

He's not your responsibility.

But he's still a human being.

Her shoulders slumped. She couldn't pretend she didn't know he was there. She had to at least check on him.

She stepped out of the canoe and tugged it up onto a muddy rise beneath some trees. Too bad he'd gone down in one of the areas unreachable by boat. She had a good, long hike ahead of her. She grabbed her walking stick, double-checked that her hunting knife was sheathed at her waist and then headed out. She hoped she wasn't making a horrible mistake. But, then again, no mistake could be worse than the one she'd already made.

Chapter Two

Dex drew a shaky breath. He was still breathing—definitely a plus. His heart was still beating, adrenaline making it pound so hard it seemed to be slamming against his rib cage. And the plane wasn't on fire—yet. Two more pluses. But the big minus was that he was hanging upside down, strapped to what was left of his seat, with jet fuel dripping down the ruined fuselage onto his shirt. And he was pretty sure he'd cut his right leg, since sharp pain shot up his calf every time he tried to maneuver his foot out of the tangled mass of metal above him.

His main concern was the jet fuel. The noxious smell made it difficult to breathe. But more worrisome was that if any of the fuel made contact with the hot engine, he was going to go up like a human torch. He had to get out of the plane and out of his fuel-soaked shirt.

Without taking off his seat belt, he couldn't

reach his trapped leg to free it. But he didn't want to unclip the belt and fall to the ground. No telling what damage that might do to his leg or what he might land on. He tilted his head up—or down, depending on how he looked at it—to see what was beneath him.

The plane had gone sideways and then turned over as it went down. A massive tree had peeled the top back like a can of tuna before dumping him and the Cessna onto the ground below. He supposed he should be grateful to that tree, since it had slowed his descent and saved him from diving nose first into the mud. The thick, now-broken branches had cushioned the fall and were now suspending the cockpit a few feet above the mud. All in all it was a miracle that he'd survived.

The muddy grass a few feet beneath his head appeared to be clear of debris. If he could work his leg free he could drop down without doing too much more damage. He used his free leg to kick at the metal trapping his right foot. Once, twice, three times. Another sharp pain in his calf was the price of freedom as the metal snapped and broke away. He pulled his knees up to his chest, put his left hand over his head to protect himself, then released his seat belt. He dropped and rolled, coming to rest on his backside.

He hurriedly shed his shirt and tossed it toward the plane as he shoved himself to his feet. After a quick look around to assess his surroundings, which basically consisted of cypress trees and saw grass, he clopped through the semi-firm ground to the one body of water he could see—a large puddle. Whenever it rained he imagined this whole area would probably be underwater. Right now it was a mixture of soft dirt and soggy bog. He dropped to his knees and sniffed the water to make sure it wasn't jet fuel. The putrid smell wasn't pleasant but at least it was biological, not man-made.

Hating the necessity of it, he cupped the water and used it to scrub his arms and chest and as much of his back as he could reach, ridding himself of the dangerous jet fuel that had coated his torso. Then he sat and yanked his pant leg up to see what, if anything, he could do about his injuries. Blood smeared his skin, but after washing it away he wasn't all that worried. The bleeding had mostly stopped and the cuts didn't look too deep. Except for one small puncture wound, mostly his leg had just been scraped, no worse than skinning a knee.

He dropped his pant leg into place. Now that he was out of danger of being roasted alive, time for his second priority. Getting the heck out of Dodge. He pulled his cell phone out of the clip on his waistband and sent up a silent prayer that the phone wasn't broken as he typed his pass code to unlock it. But a few minutes later, after turning in every direction, holding the phone up above his head, then down toward the ground, the screen still showed the same thing.

Zero bars. No service. *Useless.*

He shoved it in the holder. Might as well face what he'd so far been avoiding. He drew his gaze up to his plane and groaned. Even though he'd known it was beyond being salvaged from what he'd glimpsed while hanging from the pilot's seat, seeing the whole thing now was devastating.

The fixed landing gear pointed up at the sky. One wing was completely sheared off. He didn't see it anywhere. The other, still attached, was snared in a pile of broken branches. The tail had snapped off and had landed in the mud behind the fuselage. He shook his head in disgust. Not because of the money this would cost him. He could easily absorb the loss. But to see a piece of beautiful machinery destroyed like that was akin to a Monet being wadded up and tossed in the trash. It was a damn shame, a waste.

He shaded his eyes and looked up at the sky, a beautiful, bright blue unmarred by clouds, with no sign of the mysterious mist that had engulfed the plane right before the engine died. Even if his Mayday call hadn't gone through, that sky would still soon be dotted with other planes, or helicopters, searching the marsh for him. Because even though he was often lazy about filing flight plans, his assistant religiously checked behind him and would have insured the plan was submitted.

Yes, instead of heading straight to the Naples airport and then driving from there to Mystic Glades, he'd made a slight detour to get an aerial view of Mystic Glades first. But that had only taken him a few miles out of his planned flight path. As long as the transponder in his plane was working, a rescue crew would be able to zero in on his location.

Transponder. *Was* it working? It was part of the instrument panel that had gone on the fritz. But the system had built-in redundancies to insure it could survive most crashes and send out a signal if it received a ping from a transmitter, like the kind a rescue plane would send. He studied the wreckage, looking for any telltale signs of smoke. There were none. After waiting a few more minutes, he decided to chance a closer look. It should be safe, as long as he kept an eye out for any warning signs of an impending fire—and stayed away from the jet fuel.

He worked his way to the cockpit, approaching from the far side this time since it seemed fuel-free there. The instrument panel was a disaster. No way to tell if the transponder was working or not. If it wasn't, that was more of an inconvenience than a concern. It wasn't like he was in an uninhabited area. Mystic Glades couldn't be more than two, three miles away.

Of course, the trick was making sure he headed in the right direction. But he could use the sun to figure out which way to go. Navigating by sun or stars was a rusty skill, but one that had been ingrained in him during his pilot training in the navy. Still, there was no point in risking getting lost if a rescue effort was under way. Which, based on the anticipated arrival time in his flight plan, should be soon.

Knowing the National Transportation Safety Board would immediately take possession of the plane and site for their investigation into the cause of the crash, he figured he might as well take advantage of his time alone to do some of his own investigating.

Getting to the engine compartment wasn't as difficult as he'd anticipated, since the access panels had been peeled back like the top of the plane. Since the plane was upside down, he ducked down and looked for anything obvious. Most of the engine was intact. Only a few parts had been ripped away or crushed on impact. Everything looked normal.

Except for the electrical tape.

What the…? There were two long pieces of tape, or rather, one long piece that had been burned in two. He pulled out his cell phone and took some pictures, then zoomed the screen. Wait, no, that couldn't be. He shoved the phone in its holder.

Bracing himself on a twisted piece of metal, he followed the piece of tape. One end was attached to the edge of the engine compartment. The other was wrapped around a bundle of wires—a crucial bundle that provided power to instrument panels, including the transponder and the engine. Someone had pulled those wires free of their normal harness and used the tape to hold them in place. Which pretty much guaranteed that during flight, with the heat and vibration from the engine, the tape would fail. The wires would have dropped down onto the hot manifold. If the heat seared through their protective coating, that would have caused a catastrophic failure. Judging by the burn spots on the wires, that's exactly what had happened.

Since electrical tape wasn't standard equipment in any engine compartment, especially a brand-new plane, he could only reach one logical conclusion.

Someone had tried to kill him.

AMBER CROUCHED BEHIND a large fern that protected her from the sharp ends of a massive saw palmetto, totally mesmerized by the way the sun slanted off the golden skin of the impressive male specimen thirty feet away. She didn't know why he'd taken off his shirt, but she certainly wasn't complaining. The way his muscles rippled beneath his skin as he walked was fascinating, and an amusing contrast to his dark blue dress pants and expensive-looking but thoroughly ruined dress shoes. Since his footprints were the only ones she'd found after she'd reached the plane crash site, he must be the pilot. And the lack of bodies in and around the plane reassured her that no one else had been onboard. No one had died.

But based on how he was limping, she wasn't sure that would hold true for long.

His right leg seemed to be the one that he was favoring. From the rips in his pants, she assumed he'd been hurt during the crash and wasn't just suffering from some kind of disability. Unfortunately, the smears of mud on his back and chest meant that he may have washed himself in one of the brackish pools of water near the plane. If he'd done the same to his injuries, he might have introduced some nasty bacteria into his system. People who got lost in the Glades tended to succumb to exposure or infection just as often as other causes. If he didn't get medical attention soon, he might become one of those statistics.

So far he was heading in the right direction, toward Mystic Glades. As long as he continued that way, he'd reach town before nightfall. Her former townspeople might not exactly welcome strangers, but they would never turn away someone in need. Whoever was running The Moon these days would have some kind of medicine or potion to treat him. Or maybe Freddie would drive him to the nearest hospital in her ancient Cadillac, assuming the thing was still running. Either way, the pilot would get the help he needed. There was no reason for Amber to let him see her. All she had to do was keep following him, and somehow steer him if he went off course.

SOMEONE WAS FOLLOWING HIM.

Normally, Dex would have called out to whoever was hiding in the bushes, padding after him in the mud, keeping a good thirty or forty feet back, from what he could figure. But that was before he'd realized someone was trying to kill him. Knowing *that* had changed his perspective a hundred-eighty degrees.

He couldn't imagine his nemesis—whoever that might be—calculating the exact location where he might be when the wires in his Cessna burned through. There were too many variables for that. But it hadn't exactly been a secret at the office that he was flying to Naples, and that he was going to then drive up to Mystic Glades. Maybe whoever wanted him six feet under had planted someone near Mystic Glades to finish him off if their plan failed and he didn't crash. Or, in this case, if he *did* crash and the impact didn't kill him.

A faint crackling noise sounded behind him, like a twig breaking in half. He pretended not to notice and kept going. He needed to wait until he was near a larger clump of trees instead of just the small groupings he was passing now as he slogged through the marshy grasses. Then he'd catch his pursuer.

Just thinking about someone hiding out here like a coward to attack him was pissing him off. That and this awful heat. He wiped sweat from his brow, surprised to find his hand wet enough to shake off droplets. When had it gotten this hot? Yeah, it was probably around noon, but still, the cooling marsh breezes had been comfortable an hour ago when he'd started on this trek. Now it was as if someone had turned the sun up twenty degrees and was trying to cook him.

His shirt. That had to be it. Without his shirt to protect him from the sun, he was baking out here. Maybe he should sit in the shade for a few minutes and cool off. No, not with someone following him. He had to take care of that problem first. Then he'd sit and cool off.

A group of trees about thirty feet ahead looked like the perfect place to catch his follower unaware. The trees suddenly wavered and shifted. What the...? He stopped, wiped more sweat from his brow and shook his head. He blinked a few times until the trees stopped dancing around. The heat. It had to be the heat. He idly leaned down and rubbed the growing ache in his right leg, then wobbled forward.

He reached the trees and ducked behind the largest one and then crouched down to wait. He pulled out his cell phone, ready to snap a picture when his pursuer came into view, figuring that if he lost this upcoming battle at least there'd be a picture of his attacker for police to find later. It would be a small victory to hold on to as he breathed his last breath. For some reason, that seemed funny—in addition to being pathetic—and he almost laughed out loud, just barely keeping it together, reminding himself he couldn't risk alerting his prey.

His prey? Right. When had he ever been a hunter? This time he couldn't contain his laughter. He clamped his hand over his mouth but changed his mind when he started to lose his balance. He grabbed a low-hanging branch on the tree beside him and kept his phone in his right hand, poised to snap his all-important picture.

Good grief, it was hotter than Hades. His friend Jake was a fool to want to live here.

Half-dried mud crunched like sand beneath someone's feet. Dex leaped out from behind the tree, snapping pictures.

No one was there.

He shifted and heard the crunching sound again. He looked down, wiggled his toes in his shoes. Crunch. Wiggle. Crunch. Wait. Was that him making that noise?

A shadow shifted beside him. He whirled around, snapping pictures as he fell to the ground. The shadow became a beautiful woman standing over him, her face mirroring concern. As she reached out a delicate-looking hand, he snapped another picture, then let his hands fall to his sides. All his strength had strangely drained away.

Her blessedly cool hand touched his brow.

It felt so good he pushed his head against her palm.

"You're burning up," she said.

He blinked until he could focus on her face. His breath caught. "Canoe Girl! I waved at you." He frowned and waggled his finger. "You didn't wave back."

"I...must not have seen you. Sorry."

"No worries. I'm Dex. But you can just call me Dex."

"O...kay. Dex. Let's take a look at that leg of yours."

He grinned up at her. "Honey, you can look at anything you want."

She rolled her eyes and moved to his right leg. He lifted his head to watch, but it felt so heavy he dropped it back down.

"Ouch." He rubbed his head, wondering why it suddenly hurt.

Cool air rushed against his heated skin as she pulled his pant leg up.

"Hey, Canoe Girl. What's your name?"

"Canoe Girl works." She drew in a sharp breath. "I'm guessing you didn't have these red lines going up and down your calf before the crash."

"Nope." He dropped his phone and used both hands to lift his heavy head to look at her. "I'm guessing that's a bad thing?"

She nodded. "Could be. If not treated right away." She looked past him. "No one in Mystic Glades knows how to treat something like this, unless things have changed."

"Unless things have changed? You don't live there, Canoe Girl?"

"Um, no." She pushed his pant leg down.

"But you're familiar with it. You *used* to live there?"

She shot him a look. He should have known what that look meant, but her face went out of focus and he closed his eyes.

"Do you have any medicine in your plane?" she asked.

"Nope. Fresh out. Where do you live, beautiful?"

"That must be one bad fever." She brushed her hands on her shorts and stood. "We've got to get you to Mystic Glades. Someone there will take you to the hospital. Come on." She held her hand out to him.

He frowned, not at all pleased. "Do I have to get up? It's kind of comfy down here. It would be even more comfy if you lay down with me."

"No, thanks. We need to get moving. Come on." She grasped his hand.

He sighed heavily and tugged his hand out of hers. "I'll do it by myself. You're a tiny little thing. I wouldn't want to hurt you." He rolled over and forced himself up on his knees. A pair of surprisingly strong arms grabbed him around his waist and helped him stand. He staggered and she pulled his right arm around her shoulders, keeping her other arm around his waist.

Impressed, he smiled down at her and patted the top of her head. "You're stronger than you look, little one."

"And you don't smell anywhere near as good as *you* look. So let's get this over with."

He let out a crack of laughter. "Now that's one I've never heard before. My apologies. I think it's eau de jet fuel mixed with eau de swamp water."

She didn't respond. All in all, his little rescuer didn't seem to have much of a sense of humor. Too bad. Making a woman smile, seeing joy light up her eyes, was one of his greatest pleasures. Especially when they were making love.

The infernal heat seemed worse now. And the growing stiffness in his leg was making walking more and more of a chore. Even with Canoe Girl's help, his steps were growing slower and slower. He stumbled and grabbed a tree for support.

"You can do it," she urged, pulling him back from the tree.

"Actually, I'm not sure that I can. How much farther do we have to go?"

"A hundred yards, give or take."

He squinted at the wavering shapes in front of him then gave her an admonishing look. "You're teasing me. I don't see any buildings. It must be farther than that to Mystic Glades."

"It's a hundred yards to my *canoe*. Make it there and I can take you the rest of the way to town."

A wave of dizziness had him grabbing another tree. "I don't...think I can...make it that far."

"Sure you can. What are you, six-two? You're a big, strong guy. Just put one foot in front of the other. Close your eyes if it makes it easier."

He took a shaky step. "I don't suppose you have a four-wheeler hidden behind a tree somewhere closer than the canoe?"

"I'm fresh out of four-wheelers today."

"Bummer. I would have liked to ride a four-wheeler, especially with a pretty girl. Everything's better with a pretty girl." He winked and tried to grin, but the effort required more energy than he had left. "So...tired." He fell to his knees and surrendered to the darkness.

Chapter Three

Amber groaned and sank to her knees beside the handsome stranger with the corny yet kind of endearing sense of humor. Eau de jet fuel? If she hadn't been so worried about his fever she might have laughed at that. And she couldn't remember the last time she'd laughed.

Now that he was unconscious, how was she supposed to help him? Even though her canoe was a short jog away, it might as well have been miles. There was no way she could drag him that far. And even though he certainly wasn't packing any extra pounds, all those scrumptious-looking muscles had to amount to a lot of weight.

She pressed her hand to his forehead again and grimaced. He was like a furnace. If she didn't get his fever down soon he might have a seizure. And those red lines on his leg meant he had blood poisoning. That was probably what was causing the fever. That kind of infection could easily kill him no matter how big and strong he was.

She pulled his phone out of her pocket. When he'd dropped it earlier, she'd picked it up, planning on erasing the pictures he'd taken of her before returning the phone to him. But right now she just wanted to see if she could call for help, even though odds were high there wasn't any reception out here. When she'd made the swamp her home, she'd had a cell phone but had quickly learned that it was useless in about 99 percent of the Glades. She did know a few spots that got reliable reception, but they were much deeper into the swamp, too far away to be of use right now.

She pressed the main button and it asked her for her password. Shoot. She should have asked him for the code while he was delirious with fever and still conscious. He might have told her without a second thought. The service bars showed No Service anyway, so there was really no point. Making a call had been a long shot.

She shoved it into her pocket.

So, what now? Getting him to the canoe would take hours, assuming she could roll him there, which was the only way she could think of moving him. But she didn't think he had hours, not with that kind of fever. She had to bring it down. But how? Medicine, even if she could bring herself to try to doctor someone again, would take too long to make—and that was only if she could find the right plants. What she really needed was a bag of ice, something not exactly around every corner out here.

Wait. She might not have ice, but she had access to the next best thing. A spring. There were a handful of them scattered throughout the Glades, feeding ice-cold fresh water into the marsh from deep underground aquifers. And there were a few close by, one of them much closer than her canoe. It was worth a try. But how to get him there?

Her gaze dropped to his belt. Yes. That might work. She unbuckled it and worked it free, rolling him to pull it from underneath him. Then she strapped it around his chest below his arms and fastened it on the last hole. His chest was wide and muscular. It didn't give her much play in the belt, but it gave her enough to be able to slip her hands beneath his back and grasp the belt. She was just short enough that this might work.

Bracing her legs wide apart, she heaved backward. He slid easier than she'd expected on the soft mud and she almost fell on her rear end. Through a series of trial and error she finally found the best angle and managed to get him moving at a decent clip. She pulled him around the group of trees toward the spring, which was only thirty feet behind her, hidden in another group of trees. The muscles in her arms burned and her back was aching by the time she'd gotten him just ten feet from their original location.

She had to stop and take deep breaths, letting her shaking muscles rest before she started up again. Any hope that she might be able to use this method to get him to the canoe died a quick death. It would be a miracle if she could just get him to the freshwater. Someone had died once because of her actions. She was determined not to let her inaction be the cause of this man's death. Giving up wasn't an option. She had to keep going.

Fifteen minutes later she finally had him beside the spring, next to a shallow spot where she could sit and hold him without him slipping in too far and drowning. She emptied his pockets of his wallet and keys, leaving them up on the bank. After shucking his shoes and her boots, along with her knife, she took a bracing breath, then slid into the spring.

She gasped and pressed her hands against her breasts, her teeth already chattering even though she was barely covered by the water as she sat down. Shivering violently, she grabbed the belt around Dex and tugged, hard.

He slipped easily over the soft side and she had to grab his head to keep it above water as his body rolled over. She caught his face against her chest, mortified when his hands came up around her and he pressed his face harder into the valley between her breasts. His eyes, however, were still closed, which was the only reason she didn't slap him.

"He doesn't know what he's doing," she reminded herself as she grabbed his shoulders and pushed up with her knees to flip him onto his back.

His body settled against hers in the V of her legs and she wrapped her hands under his armpits and around his chest, holding him tightly so he didn't slide beneath the water. She lay back against the edge of the bank, her teeth chattering so hard they clicked against each other. But it didn't take long for the incredible heat of his body to begin transferring to her.

He was still so alarmingly hot that she was actually sweating where his head rested against her breasts, in spite of the chill bumps on the rest of her skin. She cupped the cold water and dribbled it on his hair and his face, getting as much of him wet as possible. She continued putting cold water on his hair, his forehead, his neck, all while trying to monitor both of their temperatures. If she ended up with hypothermia, they'd both be in trouble.

She clung to him, freely plastering her body against his to warm herself while keeping him covered in the cold water. All the while she continued to rub the water into his scalp and on his skin.

When her hands and feet started going numb and she started feeling drowsy, she knew she had to get out of the spring. But he was still warm. Not as burning hot as before, thank goodness, but far too warm to be out of danger. She edged out of the water, pulling on the belt to tug him with her. She sat cross-legged on the bank, her skin covered with goose bumps. She managed to pull him half out of the water, keeping her hands locked under the belt to keep him from sliding back in. His rear end and legs were still in the water. Hopefully, that would be enough to continue bringing his fever down while she warmed up for a few minutes in the sun.

When the feeling had returned to her extremities and she was no longer shaking, she slid into the water with him, submerging all of him except his head and going through the same routine all over again.

She repeated the process for what had to

be over an hour before he finally began to show real signs of improvement. Instead of the ruddy, red complexion that showed he was in the grips of the fever, the color drained away and he became more pale. When his skin pebbled with goose bumps, he moaned and tried to twist away from her.

She ruthlessly held on to him, determined to make sure his fever was gone before she'd let him out of the water. Unable to let him go for fear he'd drown, she pressed her cheek against the side of his face to see how hot he was. Still warmer than he should be, but so much better than before that it barely counted.

He suddenly jerked away from her and rolled over, pressing her down into the water. She just managed to grab a lungful of air before she went under. He followed her down, his body on top of hers, his eyes—a startling green—were open and staring at her in confusion as he held his breath and held her down.

His hands grabbed her waist and he pulled back, suddenly lifting her out of the water against his chest as he smoothly stepped up on the bank. She clung to his shoulders, amazed he was so strong after seeming so weak earlier. Water cascaded off both of them as he dropped to the ground with her still in his arms. Whether by design or accident—she wasn't sure—he'd managed to position her so that she was straddling him. And from the widening of his eyes and the sudden movement of him beneath her, he wasn't unaffected by the intimacy of their position.

"Let me go." She smacked at his hands and shoved his chest.

He blinked, then a slow grin spread across his face. "Canoe Girl. I thought you were a dream."

"More like a nightmare," she grumbled. "Let me go."

"I like you right where you are."

So did she. And that was the problem. The spring had done a good job of washing away the stench of the bog he'd bathed in earlier. And up close like this, just inches from his face, she couldn't deny just how devastatingly handsome he was. Add to that how long it had been since she'd even seen a good-looking man, much less done anything else, and it was almost impossible to resist the urge to wiggle against his growing erection beneath her.

Good grief. Maybe she was the one with the fever now. He was a stranger. An incredibly *hot* one, even when he wasn't running a temperature, but still a stranger.

He frowned. "Why are you all wet?"

She choked at his unintended double entendre and coughed to cover her embarrassment.

"We're, ah, both wet. From the spring." She waved her hand toward the water behind them. "You had a fever and I put you in the cold water to bring it down. Now, if you'll please—"

"If you insist." He yanked her against his chest and brought his mouth down on hers.

She was so startled she didn't immediately pull back. And by the time she thought to do so, he was kissing her senseless and her brain shut down. She slid her hands up his bare chest and around his neck, pressing herself against him as she opened her mouth for his searching tongue. He groaned and fell back against the bank, pulling her with him, deepening the kiss.

A sinfully long time later they broke apart, each of them gasping for breath.

He framed her face in his hands. "You're so beautiful."

"So are you."

He laughed and they reached for each other again.

Kissing him was insane. Crazy. Stupid. And *wonderful*. She'd never, ever been kissed like this before. Every tug of his lips on hers, every swirl of his tongue inside her mouth sent an answering pull straight to her belly.

Stop. This isn't just crazy, it's wrong. He's

probably still delirious. He doesn't know what he's doing.

She whimpered, hating her conscience but knowing it was right. If the roles were reversed, she'd be appalled and feel that he'd taken advantage of her.

Shoving against his chest, she broke the kiss and sat back. "We have to stop. This isn't—"

His eyes closed and he collapsed onto his back.

"—right," she finished, then frowned. "Dex?" She shook him. "Dex?" When he didn't respond, she scrambled off his lap and checked his breathing. He was breathing deeply, evenly. His pulse was strong. But he was definitely unconscious.

Alarmed, she pulled his right pant leg up again and drew a sharp breath. "Oh, no." The red streaks were worse, much worse. And they extended well past his knee now.

She shook him. "Dex, wake up. Come on. Dex."

He moaned, as if in pain, but his eyes stayed shut.

Amber sat back, chewing her bottom lip. There was only one thing she knew that might help him, a potion she could make by mixing mud and two specific plants together into a poultice to draw out the poison. But what if she remembered wrong? What if she did more harm than good?

He moaned again, his handsome face scrunching up in a grimace.

If she didn't help him, he'd die. Of that she was sure. The poultice was his only hope.

Please help me remember how to mix it right.

She shoved to her feet, grabbed her knife from the pile of belongings on the bank and took off running.

Chapter Four

Dex twisted against the sheets, fighting through the darkness.

A delicate face leaned over him, her long, brown hair forming a curtain, her brow furrowed with concern.

"Sleep, Dex. Don't worry. I'll watch over you. You're getting better."

He reached for her. "Don't go, Canoe Girl." *But she faded away like a ghost.*

He cursed and tried to roll over, but every movement was painful. His entire body ached, as if he was back in college and had been in a drunken fraternity fistfight—and had lost.

A cool cloth stroked his arms, his forehead, driving back the awful heat that seemed to constantly surround him. Voices he didn't recognize whispered close by. Footsteps echoed and a door slammed. A glass was held to his lips. He drank greedily and the cool water soothed his parched throat.

Canoe Girl leaned over him again. No, she was sitting this time, raising her arms, then lowering them, over and over, her muscles bunching with strain. She raised her hands, pulling something up into the air. Water dripped from it onto his pants. An oar? Why was she holding an oar? She moved it to the other side and dipped down again.

And then she was on her knees in front of him, her cool fingers brushing against his brow. That worried frown a constant twin to the look of concern in her eyes. Sad eyes. So, so sad.

She slid her arms around his neck and hugged him close. "Don't tell them about me, Dex. Please. Don't tell."

"I won't. I swear."

He thrashed against the sheets, seeking relief from the heat. Hot. He was always so hot. He couldn't remember *not* being hot.

The darkness called to him again and he gratefully surrendered.

DEX OPENED HIS EYES, blinking at the light.

"Well it's about time you decided to rejoin the living. I was beginning to think the doc was wrong."

He turned his head on the pillow to see a woman nearly as brawny as him, probably well over twice his age, with falsely bright red hair, sitting in a ladder-back chair beside the bed. He looked around the room but she was the only one there. "Where am I?"

"Callahan's Watering Hole, in the extra bedroom in my apartment upstairs. I'm Freddie Callahan."

"From Mystic Glades?"

"Either I'm famous and didn't know it or our buddy Jake told you about me."

He frowned. "How would you know that I know Jake?"

"I saw your last name on your ID, in your wallet. Figured it was too much of a coincidence for you to be named Lassiter and not be from Lassiter and Young Private Investigations. Called Jake—which was a pain since I had to leave town to get reception—and sure enough, he vouched for you."

He started to scoot up in the bed but stopped when he realized he was naked beneath the sheet. He yanked it higher before sitting up. The room was small, with only the narrow bed, a dresser and a single window. A collection of shot glasses and empty whiskey bottles sat on a shelf along the far wall. And a pair of open doors beneath them revealed a closet and a small bathroom. He tried to remember how he'd gotten there, but his mind was a haze of confusing images and impressions.

"I'm sorry," he said. "But I don't—"

"Remember what happened?" Freddie patted his hand. "No worries. We pretty much pieced everything together with Jake's help after I called him. You crashed your plane into the Glades. The airplane folks done packed up what was left of it onto some fancy barge and took it with them to Naples for some kind of investigation. You got an infection and have been unconscious for a while. I had Doc Holliday come out and check on you to make sure you were coming along okay. You're gonna be just fine."

"Doc Holliday?"

Her mouth cracked open in a gap-toothed grin. "I've called him that for so long that I don't remember his real name anymore. He's a city slicker, comes out to the Glades when we have an emergency. He wanted to take you back to town, but Jake and I told him you were family and I kept you here in Mystic Glades. Jake said he'd call your people in Saint Augustine and tell them where you were. Ain't nobody been by to check on you yet, though, which just proves we made the right decision keeping you here."

She crossed her arms and gave him a crisp

nod, as if to let him know she wasn't impressed with his family's lack of concern. Of course, she had no way of knowing that the only reason his family would come was if they thought he was already dead and they stood a chance of getting their hands on his money.

A pounding started in his temple as he tried to think back to what had happened. Electrical tape. He'd found it in the engine compartment. Maybe it was a good thing that no one had shown up looking for him in Mystic Glades. Without knowing who'd tampered with his plane, he wasn't sure whom he could trust.

Images of the crash and its aftermath filtered through his mind: cutting his leg, waking to find himself in a freezing cold spring, a beautiful young woman helping him out of a canoe and onto the bank.

"Don't tell them about me, Dex. Please. Don't tell."

He scrubbed the stubble on his face and searched the corners of the room again, part of him hoping she'd be there even though he knew she wouldn't be.

Freddie's expression turned introspective as she studied him. "You're looking for the woman who helped you, aren't you? The one you call Canoe Girl?"

Canoe Girl. He squeezed his eyes shut. He

remembered it all now. She'd put some kind of foul-smelling mud on his leg—to draw out the poison, she'd told him. And when he'd alternated between the fever and bone-rattling chills, she'd built a fire and sat with him all night, leaving only to bring him water and some kind of surprisingly delicious stew.

Every hour, without fail, she'd changed the dressing on his leg. And when he'd needed a moment of privacy and, to his shame, was unable to get up on his own, she'd helped him stand and limp to a clump of bushes. When he was done, she'd escorted him to their little campfire.

She'd entertained him with stories about the Everglades and made him laugh when she spoke about her childhood. He'd told her about flying and about later building his empire, only to become bored and start the PI firm with Jake Young for fun.

When the sun came up he'd awakened to find her curled against him beside the dying campfire. In awe of the beautiful creature, he'd tightened his arms, only to find her blinking at him in surprise and slipping out of his grasp. Far too soon, she'd deemed him strong enough to leave and had helped him limp to her canoe.

After taking him to the woods at the edge of

town, she'd helped him sit on a fallen log and crouched down in front of him.

"We're just a few feet from the main road," she whispered. She pulled a whistle out of her pocket. "When I blow this, someone will come help you." She slid her arms around his neck and hugged him close. "Don't tell them about me, Dex. Please. Don't tell. Make up some kind of story to explain how you got here, but never tell anyone that you saw me. It's important."

The fear in her voice had him clutching both of her shoulders and pulling her back so he could look her in the eyes. "What's going on? Who are you afraid of?"

"It's…complicated. Please. Just promise me."

"Okay. Yes, I promise. But tell me why you're afraid. I'm sure that I can help—"

She pressed her fingers against his lips to stop him. "No one can help me." Her mouth quirked up in a rare smile. "Not even a sexy navy pilot turned billionaire financier private investigator." She stood and backed away, then put the whistle to her lips.

The shrill sound shattered the morning, sending birds shrieking and rising from the trees around them.

"Remember your promise." She turned and disappeared into the woods.

Dex shook his head to clear his thoughts. Freddie sat across from him, still waiting for his answer. A feeling of impending doom settled over him. If he'd kept his promise, then how did this woman know about Canoe Girl?

"My memory is still a bit…foggy," he said evasively. "How long have I been here?"

"Three days. Doc said you wouldn't have made it if Amber hadn't helped you with that concoction she put on your leg. But still, it was touch and go."

"Amber?"

"Amber Callahan. My niece, the one you called Canoe Girl when you were delirious. Pretending you don't know who I'm talking about isn't going to change the fact that you talked quite a bit about her."

He fisted his hands in the sheets, guilt and shame settling on top of him like a heavy weight. Canoe Girl—Amber—had saved his life. And, in return, all she'd asked was that he not tell anyone about her. He'd betrayed her, whether he'd meant to or not.

"They're searching for her. Now that we know she's nearby, Holder and the others won't stop until they find her trail and bring her back."

His stomach twisted into a hard knot. "She doesn't want to be found."

"I'm sure you're right."

He frowned. For an aunt, she didn't seem all that worried about her niece's welfare. "Then why is this Holder person searching for her? It's her right to be left alone if that's what she wants. If he thinks she needs rescuing, believe me, she's quite capable of taking care of herself. She's pretty amazing in that department."

She gave him a peculiar look, as if she thought he'd lost his mind. "Mr. Lassiter, Deputy Holder isn't leading a rescue party. He's leading a posse. Amber is a murderer."

Chapter Five

Amber ducked down behind a trash can against the back of Callahan's Watering Hole and waited for the newest group of men to get out of their cars and go inside. The foot traffic in and out of the bar all morning had been incredible, not to mention several suits in a limo a few minutes ago. Half the town and strangers she'd never seen before must have been inside at one time or another. And she didn't have to guess why. They were looking for her, had been for three days now, carrying rifles and shotguns as if they were afraid she'd attack them. The resentment that shot through her was like a physical pain, making her double over. These people had been her friends, her family. At one time they'd have done anything for her. Now they just wanted to put her away.

She could have been safe and sound at home deep in the Glades by now, but she couldn't stop worrying about Dex. She'd watched from a perch in a tree overhead to insure that her plan had worked—that someone heard her whistle and came to help him. And since the first person on the scene was someone she'd never met, she couldn't just assume he had good intentions as far as Dex was concerned. He could have been a thief or some such. So she'd scampered down the tree and followed him to make sure Dex didn't need her. Then she'd safely made it to her canoe and headed out. But she wasn't comfortable with the things that she'd heard when she spied on the crash site and listened to the men gathering up the plane. So she'd gone back to check on him and had made a habit of checking on him every day. Once he was well and awake and able to fend for himself, she'd quit her vigil. But not before then.

The men she'd been waiting to pass finally went inside, letting the screen door slam shut behind them. Amber waited another couple of minutes, peeking out to see if anyone else was approaching and listening for sounds from inside the bar to tell her if anyone was about to leave. Then she hurried around the trash can and raced up the rickety wooden staircase attached to the back of the building that was supposed to be a fire escape but was so rarely used that it had fallen into disrepair. The way the boards sagged as she stepped on each one had her holding her breath the first day she'd snuck up them, but now she knew they were more solid than they seemed and she no longer held her breath as she hurried up to the landing.

The door was unlocked, as always. That was one thing she could be thankful for, that the residents of Mystic Glades rarely locked their doors. She pulled the door open a fraction to peer down the long upstairs hallway with doors opening off either side. With all the people downstairs in the business part of the building, she hadn't expected her aunt to be up here in her private quarters and wasn't disappointed. The hall was empty.

She headed straight to the guest room where Dex was staying. If he was still suffering from his fever she would sit with him as she had the past few days and use a cool cloth to soothe him. She wished she could speak to the doctor who came every evening and ask him if Dex was going to be okay. But with everyone searching for her, that wasn't in the realm of possibilities.

She carefully eased the door open and hurried inside, shutting it behind her and flipping the lock. Movement to her right had her whirling around. A body slammed into her, tackling her to the floor. She landed hard, her elbows and head thumping against the wooden floor a split second before the person who'd attacked her landed on top of her. She grimaced at the pain that shot through her then blinked in surprise to see the very green, shocked gaze of Dex looking down at her. A very naked Dex, plastered to every inch of her body. And like when she'd ended up in his lap out in the swamp, his body immediately responded to their closeness and began to harden against her belly.

He cursed and rolled off her, grabbing her wrists and yanking her to her feet.

"What are you doing here?" he demanded in a harsh whisper as he pulled her to the bed.

She tried to focus on the unexpected anger in his voice, but she couldn't resist a quick look down. The parts of his body that had been hidden from her when she'd been nursing him to health were now fully revealed. And she wasn't disappointed in the least. The rest of him was just as…impressive…as his naked chest had been.

He grabbed a blanket from the foot of the bed and wrapped it around his hips. If they'd been in the swamp, he'd have made some flirty, corny comment. But the teasing flirtation she'd come to expect from him in their brief time together was replaced by a sullen, angry, serious stranger.

Her shoulders slumped. "You know."

"That you're wanted for murder? Yeah, hard to miss that topic around here. About that—I want you to know that I didn't tell them about you on purpose."

She waved her hand. "No worries. You were delirious. It's not your fault."

"How would you know I was delirious?"

She swallowed and shrugged. "A...ah, guess. I knew you still had the fever when I left you. And, since Deputy Holder headed up that posse after me so fast, they obviously knew about me. And I trust you—I know you meant it when you said you wouldn't tell. Again, no worries. Not your fault." She tugged her arm out of his hold. "It was a mistake. I'll go. I'm sorry to have troubled you."

He blocked her way. "Not so fast. There are things...we need to talk."

"No, I need to get out of here before someone catches me."

"If you're that worried, why'd you come here in the first place?"

She blinked as if remembering something, then reached into her pocket and pulled out a cell phone. "You dropped this earlier. I kept it at first to try to erase the pictures of me. But there's no point in that anymore. So...here you go." She handed it to him and he tossed it onto the bed.

"I don't think you risked everything to come here to return a phone. What's the real reason that you're here?"

She blew out a long breath. "Guilt, I guess. I was worried that I'd left you unprotected. You're obviously able to care for yourself now, so my job is done. Time to go."

"Turn around."

"What? Why?"

"Because I'm the only one naked in this room. Either you take your clothes off and we'll be naked together, or you turn around while I get dressed."

She hesitated, half wondering if he was serious.

"That was a joke, Amber. Turn around."

She sighed and turned around, listening to the sounds of drawers opening and the whisper of fabric against skin.

"Okay, you can turn around."

When she did, she was surprised to see him wearing dark gray dress slacks and a burgundy dress shirt tucked in, with a charcoal-gray-and-maroon-striped silk tie. The only thing missing was a suit jacket and he'd look at home in any boardroom. Pity. She liked him better half-covered in mud and jet fuel. He'd been a lot more fun and a lot less serious.

"Nice clothes. I can't imagine anyone around here having a suit you could borrow, though."

"They're my clothes. My assistant brought them."

"Your assistant. Okay. Well, you're obviously doing fine and you have...an assistant watching after you now, so I'll just be on my way." She scampered around him and ran to the door. But he was surprisingly fast for someone who'd just woken from a near-coma after several days and he braced his hand against the door, keeping her from being able to open it.

"Damn it, Amber. We need to talk."

The sound of voices outside the door and footsteps clomping up the wooden stairs had him breaking off. Amber's eyes widened in dismay. She turned in a circle, surveying the tiny room for a place to hide. The tiny bathroom or the closet. She chose the closet.

"Wait." Dex grabbed her arm in an unbreakable hold.

A knock sounded on the door.

"Please," she whispered, as she tried to pry his hand off her forearm. "Let me go. I'm just going to hide in the closet."

He shook his head. "No. You're not." He

half turned toward the door. "Come in," he called out.

Amber gasped in shock as the door opened. Her aunt gaped at her in surprise, then moved aside to let the group of men behind her into the room. The first two men, wearing suits much like Dex's, were strangers to her. But the last man to enter the room was not. She'd seen him two years ago, the day she'd run into the Glades.

The look of surprise on his face was quickly replaced with a look of reproach as he pulled out his handcuffs.

"Miss Callahan." Collier County Deputy Scott Holder pulled her away from Dex and turned her around. "You're under arrest for the murder of your grandfather, William Callahan."

Amber stiffened her spine while he locked the handcuffs around her wrists. Her face flamed hot as she endured the pat down with the others watching, except for Dex and one of the men in a suit who were currently deep in conversation by the window, completely ignoring her. She noted that he didn't seem surprised by the appearance of a Collier County sheriff's deputy at his door, either.

Holder took her knife and sheath from her belt. Then he escorted Amber to the door with her hands cuffed behind her back, past the admonishing look from her aunt. Dex never once looked her way.

"WELL, THIS SEEMS FAMILIAR." Deputy Holder leaned back in his desk chair in the squad room beside Dex as another officer escorted Amber into an interview room.

"Because of Faye Star?" Dex asked, noting that Amber made a point of not looking at him even though she passed less than a yard away from him.

He nodded. "Your PI partner, Jake Young, had Faye in here accused of murder just a couple of months ago. Déjà vu." He cast him a sideways glance. "Let me guess. You think Miss Callahan is innocent?"

"Honestly, I have no idea. But I certainly wasn't going to harbor a fugitive once I found out there was an outstanding warrant for her arrest. That's why I had Freddie call you to come over, so I could tell you what I knew. It was only dumb luck that she was there when you arrived."

"You're supposedly worried about making sure she doesn't run from the law. And yet you're offering your own lawyer to defend her." He nodded at Garreth Jackson as he passed them and went into the interview room.

"She saved my life. I figure the least I can do is make sure she gets a good attorney. Garreth was a criminal defense lawyer before he turned to business law. He can at least advise her until I can bring in someone else."

Holder snorted. "Sounds to me like you're going to a lot of trouble—and expense—for someone you aren't sure is innocent."

"Like I said. She saved my life. I can't put a price on that. Whatever she needs, I intend to provide it. What about you? Do you think she's guilty?"

The interview room door closed and Holder flipped the file open on top of his desk. "Seems pretty cut-and-dried. Her grandfather was the founder of Mystic Glades. He lived in a mansion, of sorts, several miles outside the town proper, with only one other person—Amber Callahan. She was known more or less as the town healer, for lack of a better term. If someone was sick or broke a bone, they went to Amber instead of taking the long drive to Naples. She was the only one with her grandfather the night he died, admitted as much the next morning when she called the police to report his death."

"Her aunt said the old man had been poisoned?"

"Poisoned? Not exactly, but close. He was

sick with the flu or something similar and she gave him one of her potions to supposedly help him sleep better. But the potion was laced with peanut oil, something he was highly allergic to. Coroner said his throat closed up and he died of anaphylactic shock. Amber knew about his allergies. Everyone did. And since she was the one who brought groceries and did all the cooking, it's kind of hard to say anyone else brought the peanut oil into the house."

"Did you actually find a bottle of peanut oil?"

He flipped the few pages in the folder and shook his head. "Nope. She must have disposed of it. But the CSU team tested the glass beside his bedside table and found peanut oil residue."

"What did she have to gain by killing him?"

"Plenty. Since he founded Mystic Glades, he pretty much owned the town and leased most of the property to others. Very few of the residents actually own the land or the buildings on them. He was quite wealthy in his own right—old money that's been in his family for generations."

"And Amber is the only heir?"

"Her and her aunt Fredericka. But Amber got the lion's share."

"Is the estate still in escrow?"

He tapped one of the pages. "No, but it might as well be. As soon as Miss Callahan was charged, the courts put holds on both her accounts and her grandfather's accounts. She can't touch a penny without going to court to release the funds."

"Which of course she wouldn't do if she's worried about being arrested for murder."

"Exactly."

Dex blew out a long breath. "I just can't picture her purposely killing her grandfather even if she did want his money. She seems so—"

"Sweet? Nice?"

"I was thinking intelligent, actually. How old was her grandfather?"

"I see where you're going." He thumbed through the report, then flipped to the beginning and ran his finger down a paragraph. "Let's see. Amber was twenty-two, her grandfather was just shy of eighty at the time. He wasn't in the best of health, either, even without having the flu at the time he died. You're thinking she could have just waited and inherited."

"Seems like the logical thing to do. Does that report say why she might have needed the money? Had she planned on leaving Mystic Glades?"

He closed the file. "The report doesn't really say much more than what I told you. Everything I've said was available through old media reports or word of mouth in Mystic, so I haven't given away any secrets. But the rest of the file *is* confidential and I can only release it to her attorney."

"Fair enough. I'm curious about one thing, as long as it's not one of those secrets you mentioned."

"Doesn't hurt to ask."

"You said the grandfather lived in a mansion. What happened to it?"

"The court apportioned some of the estate for the house's upkeep and appointed a trustee to look after the house. And before you ask, no, I can't share the trustee's name because I don't know if that's common knowledge."

Dex raised a brow. "I imagine it takes a lot of money to maintain a large house, especially in an environment like the Everglades. That trustee probably has access to a very generous bank account."

Holder shrugged. "Your words. Not mine."

"I know what it costs to maintain a large estate. I don't guess I really need your answer to that question. It does, however, make me wonder if the trustee could be culpable in the murder."

"In a normal murder case, I might agree

with you. But in this one, there's one fact you can't explain away."

"Which is?"

"Amber herself, in the interview the morning her grandfather was found dead, admitted she was the only other person in the house. She said no one else had been there for weeks. Kind of hard to argue that someone else might have killed the old man when she swore no one else had been there."

Dex was inclined to agree with him, but somehow saying that out loud would have made him feel like a traitor to the woman who had worked so hard to save him. He owed her the benefit of the doubt and was determined to keep an open mind.

The door to the interview room popped open and Garreth stepped outside, closing the door behind him. He stopped in front of the desk. "Miss Callahan has decided to retain my services until I can help her interview and hire a criminal case attorney. I'll need a copy of the original police report."

Holder held the folder up. "I figured you might. Keep it. I'll print myself a new copy."

"Thank you." He turned to Dex. "Assuming you still plan to foot the bill—"

"I do."

"Excellent. Then the calls I made in the

interview room weren't a complete waste of time. I started the ball rolling to arrange bail. Now we just have to wait for a judge to call us back."

Holder shook his head. "Not going to happen on a Saturday. Miss Callahan will have to cool her heels in jail until Monday, and even then, I highly doubt a judge will grant her bail. She's a proven flight risk."

Dex exchanged an amused look with his lawyer. "I think you underestimate Garreth's abilities, Detective."

Holder shrugged. "Maybe. I doubt it. I guess we'll see. But I—" The phone on his desk rang. When he saw the number on the display, he shot Garreth a frown and took the call.

Garreth gave him a smug look and turned to Dex again. "When you're done here, Miss Callahan has requested to speak with you."

Dex immediately stood but Holder signaled him to wait.

When he hung up the phone, he shook his head. "I can't believe what I just heard." He filled them in on the details.

Dex laughed and clapped Garreth on the shoulder. "You've still got it, my friend."

"I suppose this means your answer is yes, to both conditions?" Holder asked, not sounding happy at all.

"Are you kidding? This is the coolest thing to happen to me in ages. I'm all in."

"This is ridiculous," Holder muttered as he shoved out of his chair. "But I don't guess I have a choice. Hold up your right hand, and repeat after me."

Chapter Six

Amber clasped her hands beneath the table as Dex stepped into the tiny room and closed the door behind him. Her relief at seeing him, apparently unharmed, had her letting out a relieved breath.

He sat in the chair across from her and leaned his forearms on the table. "I'm surprised that you wanted to see me. I figure you have to blame me—"

"For my arrest?" She shook her head. "I was angry, at first. But I knew this day would come eventually. And I couldn't exactly expect a stranger to want to stick his neck out for me." She grabbed his hands in hers. "That's not the point, and not why I wanted to talk to you. You're in danger."

His brows arched as he looked at their joined hands before meeting her gaze. "You wanted to talk to me to warn me that I'm in danger?"

"Yes. I've only just now really put everything together in my mind and I wanted to tell you my suspicions. After I took you to Mystic Glades, I went to the crash site to erase any signs of me having been near there."

"To wipe out your footprints."

She nodded. "I didn't know what exactly you would tell everyone about how you got to town, but if you did keep your word, I didn't want any signs to prove otherwise."

"Let me make sure I understand. You came to my room every day of my fever and put cold cloths on my head and made sure that I was comfortable."

"What? That's not what I—"

"Wanted to talk about? No, obviously you didn't want me to know. But I remember someone doing that and your aunt looked at me like I was crazy when I asked her about it. So I know you were the one taking care of me far more than she was." He quirked his mouth up in a wry grin. "Thank you, by the way."

She tugged her hands but he laced his fingers with hers, trapping her. She blew out a breath in frustration. "Look, you need to take this seriously. Like I said, I went to the crash site and—"

"And you erased your footprints, again, to make sure that I didn't look bad if I'd kept my word and said I was alone after the crash and that no one helped me. Do I have that right? You were protecting me? Again?"

"Can we get to what matters please?"

"What matters to me is that everything everyone else is telling me about you makes you out to be a killer. But everything—every single thing that I've personally experienced with you—tells me the opposite. You seem to me like an intelligent, warm, caring person who puts everyone else's welfare above her own. Why aren't you berating me for telling about you helping me after I promised I wouldn't?"

"It wasn't your fault. We already discussed this. You were delirious. And it wasn't a fair promise anyway—to ask someone who doesn't know me to lie for me. I'm sorry I asked. I shouldn't have."

"You're doing it again."

She tugged her hands and this time he let them go, although seemingly reluctantly. She clasped her hands beneath the table again. "Look, Mr. Lassiter—"

"Dex." He grinned "We've slept together. I think we can use first names after that, don't you?"

She blinked. "I don't know what you think you remember, but we most certainly have not slept together."

"I'm wounded. You don't remember us lying

together beside the fire? You stayed with me all night, and we both slept, off and on." He winked.

She leaned across the table and thumped it impatiently. "Will you be serious? Please?"

"Oh, I'm always serious about…sleeping."

She threw her hands up. "I can see this is going nowhere. You might as well leave. I'll talk to that lawyer of yours again and tell him—"

"He's your lawyer now, too."

She swallowed hard. "Yes…I suppose. Ah, thank you for that. I promise that I'll pay you back one day. As soon as I can get out on bail, I'll look into a court-appointed lawyer."

"I wouldn't advise that. Garreth's one of the best around, even if he doesn't practice criminal law anymore. He'll make sure to arrange an equally competent criminal attorney. Murder charges are far too serious to skimp on representation. Florida isn't shy about sticking needles in people's arms. The death penalty is nothing to play around with."

She swallowed hard. "I hadn't even thought of that."

"Well, I have. This is serious, Amber. Your life is at stake."

"Aren't you even going to ask if I did it?"

"No."

"Why not?"

He shrugged. "Because I know that you didn't kill him. You're not built that way. You could have left me to die out in the swamp. But even though you knew it might mean getting caught and going to jail, you helped me. If you did that for a stranger, I have no doubt you would never have done anything to harm your family."

"Thank you," she whispered. "You have no idea how good it feels to have someone actually believe in me."

His smile faded. "Yeah, about that. I'm guessing your aunt Freddie hasn't exactly been supportive. She certainly doesn't strike me as someone in your court."

"Well, you can't really blame her. Grandpa was her daddy."

"And yet he left most everything to you. Not her. That seems rather telling."

She shrugged. "They never had the best relationship."

"And you were the one who took care of him every day. Did your aunt help at all?"

"You have to understand Freddie. She's one of the most supportive people out there. She'll do anything for you as long as—"

"You don't do something she doesn't approve of?"

"Pretty much. But she's a good person. She has a good heart."

"Not from where I'm standing." He looked down at his chair. "Or sitting." He grinned.

Even though she didn't feel the least bit happy right now, she couldn't help the answering smile that curved her lips. There was just something about Dex that lightened her heart and made her feel good. But of course, she couldn't let him distract her from her primary purpose. She cleared her throat and tried again.

"Listen, please. This is important. I need to tell you about the crash site."

"Let me guess. You heard the investigators talking near the engine and someone mentioned the tape in the engine compartment."

She blinked. "You knew?"

"Yep. I even took pictures. I emailed them to the NTSB after I woke up and already spoke to them. They concur, unofficially at least, that the plane appears to have been tampered with. Of course, their official report will take months, or longer."

She pressed a hand against her chest. "Well, okay, then. I thought you didn't know."

"That's why you came back every day to your aunt's, isn't it? To watch over me? To protect me?"

Her face flamed hot. "You make me sound

like a saint. Trust me. I'm not. I came back for purely selfish reasons. I didn't want another death on my conscience."

"Another death? You blame yourself for your grandfather's death?"

She nodded. "How can I not? I knew he had allergies. Obviously, I did something to cause him to die. I must have used something to gather the plants and herbs that used to have peanuts in it. Maybe I didn't wash it out good enough. Whatever, there was only one person who could have harmed him, and that was me."

Dex glanced at the door behind him, then at the glass along one wall before leaning forward. "I don't think anyone is behind that glass listening, but I can't be sure. Let's not sling around admissions of guilt," he whispered.

"But I—"

"Loved your grandfather," he said more loudly, "and would never do anything on purpose to harm him. Isn't that right?"

She frowned. "Yes, of course. But no one else was in the house."

"That you know of. Let's not talk about any of that right now. Let's talk about what matters right this minute."

"Getting you some kind of protection," she

said. "You seem to have plenty of money. I recommend hiring some bodyguards."

He chuckled. "You really aren't worried about yourself, are you?"

"Well, of course I am. I don't want to go to prison or…worse. But that will have to play out in the courts. There's nothing I can do about it right now. You, on the other hand, are in very real danger and need to be aware of it and take precautions."

"Understood. And thank you for wanting to make sure that I'm safe."

"Okay. Well. Um…thank you, for everything. I really appreciate your kindness in lending me your attorney." She held her hand out.

He chuckled again and shook her hand, squeezing her fingers before letting go. "I wish you nothing but the best, Amber Callahan."

"Maybe we'll meet again under better circumstances," she said. "Preferably not with me in prison."

He gave her a secretive look and then headed to the door. He rapped his knuckles on it and waited. The door opened and Officer Holder and the lawyer, Gareth Jackson, stood in the opening.

"Ready?" Holder asked.

"Yep." Dex backed up and let them into the small room, which seemed to become even smaller with the three large men standing on the other side of the table from Amber.

"Is someone going to tell me what's going on?" she asked.

Holder put his hands on his hips. "Looks like you lucked into an impressive lawyer, Miss Callahan. Five minutes on the phone with a judge and he's secured your release. But there are some conditions you have to agree to."

Her pulse sped up as she stared at him, feeling completely stunned. "He's granting bail?"

"He is. And Mr. Lassiter is kindly putting up the deposit."

"I...don't know what to say. Thank you."

Dex nodded. "You might want to wait until you hear the rest before thanking me."

"Yes," Holder continued. "There are two conditions the judge is imposing, and one that Mr. Lassiter is imposing in exchange for the bail deposit." He waved at Dex. "This is your show. Why don't you explain?"

Dex stepped forward and took Amber's hands between his. "My condition is that you consent to the exhumation of your grandfather's body so a new autopsy can be performed."

She jerked back in shock, but he kept her hands in his. "I don't understand. Why would you ask me that? Everyone knows he died because of his allergies, and I don't know that I have the right to approve that even if I wanted to. Wouldn't his daughter, Freddie, have to consent?"

"She already has," Garreth said from behind him. "Asking you is just a courtesy that Mr. Lassiter felt should be extended. We don't need your permission."

Dex shot him an aggravated glance before looking at her again. "I know you were close to him and I don't want you upset if we do this. But I think it's an important first step in proving your innocence."

"You really think a new autopsy might find something that the first one didn't?"

"It's possible. With your life hanging in the balance, it seems like a good idea. Don't you think?"

"O-okay. I guess."

"Excellent. Garreth will work out the details. As for the other conditions, the ones the judge is imposing, first, you can't leave town—as in Mystic Glades. You have to agree to stay there and not go back into the swamp and hide again until all of this plays out in the courts."

She couldn't believe her good luck. Of course, she would agree to that. She could easily slip away again. She'd hidden out for two years. There was no reason she couldn't go back to that life in the Glades again. She was about to agree, but then she realized there was a potentially huge downside.

"How much money did you have to put down to bail me out, Mr. Lassiter?"

"Dex," he gently corrected again. "Does it matter? As long as you don't run, I don't lose my money."

"That's what I'm worried about," she grumbled, low, so only he could hear.

He grinned again, which seemed strange to her under the circumstances, since she'd basically just admitted she planned on running. "Why are you smiling?"

"Because of the judge's second condition."

"Which is?"

"He thinks you're a flight risk, based on your history. The only way he would grant bail under these circumstances is if you're remanded into the custody of someone who will insure that you don't disappear again."

Visions of her aunt Freddie snarling at her and trading insults while she shoved a tray of food into her room and locked the door had Amber's stomach clenching. "Let me guess. My aunt?"

"Nope. This person also has to be an officer of the court."

"Officer of the court? Like a cop?"

"Exactly like a cop. Or a temporary deputy. That would work too."

The grin on his face had her wary. "O…kay. Whatever that means. So, who's my official babysitter?"

He grinned and held out his hand. "Happy to meet you. I'm temporary deputy and officer of the court, Dex Lassiter, your babysitter."

DEX STEPPED OUT of the back of the limo in front of Buddy Johnson's store—Swamp Buggy Outfitters—and waited for Amber to join him.

The deputy thing, though real, was mainly a gimmick to cover the judge if something happened. And Amber had warned Dex that the residents of Mystic Glades wouldn't roll out a welcome mat, or canoe, or whatever for him if they found out he was law enforcement, even in a temporary capacity. So for now, his newfound role would remain a secret between the two of them.

She slid across the leather seat and stepped out beside him, anxiously glancing around at the small crowds of people standing around the wooden boardwalks up and down Mystic Glades' Main Street, all of them watching Amber with a mixture of open hostility and suspicion.

"I think I may have been safer in jail."

Dex put his arm around her shoulders and pulled her against his side, enjoying the startled look she gave him, especially since she didn't pull away. "Don't worry. I'll take care of you."

Her startled look turned to aggravation and she shoved his arm off her shoulders. "I can take care of myself. Have been for quite a while now." She started to turn away, but he grabbed her hand and refused to let it go.

"Are you forgetting something? The conditions of your release?"

Her shoulders slumped and she quit trying to walk away. "Fine. Why are we here?" She nodded toward the store, where Buddy was now standing in the open front doorway.

A raindrop spattered onto his jacket and he glanced up at the angry clouds gathering overhead. "We're here because we need shelter, a place to stay."

"Last I heard, Buddy doesn't take on boarders. And there isn't an apartment over the store like at my aunt's anyway. I thought we were going to stay at Freddie's."

"You thought wrong." He tugged her toward the store while his driver waited inside the car. He stared at the townspeople on the boardwalk until they looked away. "I'm not about to make you stay with someone who thinks you're a murderer and makes no secret about it."

They reached the first step that led to the boardwalk and the door where Buddy was watching them with open curiosity, several of his gray-haired friends crowding the doorway behind him trying to see what was going on.

"Then where are we going to stay?" she whispered to Dex. "There isn't exactly a Holiday Inn around here."

"True. But we're not staying at a hotel." He tugged her forward with him.

"Afternoon. Mr. Johnson, isn't it? I'm Dex Lassiter." He offered his hand and was pleasantly surprised when the other man shook it. He had a much friendlier look on his face than most of the other Mystic Glades residents had.

"I know who you are. You can call me Buddy. Everyone does." His gaze settled on Amber. "It's good to see you again."

She blinked in surprise. "It is?"

"Yep. I don't believe for a minute that you had anything to do with William's death. So don't be worrying about me standing around judging you." He aimed a withering look at the same group of people that Dex had stared down moments earlier. They turned and hurried away. "I heard you made bail and that you were coming back. Have to say, I was kind of surprised. But I'm glad. I reckon you must be here for one thing—the keys to your grand-daddy's place. I stocked it up when I heard you were on your way. But you can look around inside and see if you need anything else. No charge. It's the least I can do for my best friend's granddaughter."

He waved them inside and Dex pulled a stunned Amber behind him into the store.

As Buddy went to his office to retrieve the keys to the Callahan mansion, Amber stood beside Dex in the middle of the store. The older men, friends of Buddy's, sat a short distance away on some folded-up chairs near a display of coolers and fishing poles, making no move to talk to either of them.

"I don't understand. Why does Buddy have the keys to my grandfather's house?" Amber asked. "I would have expected Freddie to have them, or at least a friend of mine, like Faye."

"Faye Star?"

Her brows rose. "You know her?"

"I know *of* her. She married my PI business partner, Jake Young. They're both out of town right now. But back to why Buddy has the keys to your grandfather's mansion. He's the execu-tor of the estate, appointed by the court to take care of the property until things with you are resolved. And before you protest that you don't want to take any supplies he may offer, trust me, they're not exactly free of charge. He's got access to a very healthy bank account to take care of that house. Plus, he receives a monthly stipend from the account for his troubles. He's been well paid."

Buddy headed down the aisle toward them, smiling as he twirled a ring of keys.

"How do you know all of this?" Amber asked.

"My attorney."

Buddy held the keys out to Dex, but Dex motioned for him to give them to Amber. "It's her house now."

Buddy's gaze shot to Dex as he handed the keys to Amber. "The charges have been dropped?"

"It's just a matter of time. You mentioned you stocked the house?"

"Um, yes, yes, I did. The pantry and refrigerator are full, even loaded up the deep freeze. You'll have to put sheets on the beds but all of that is there, too. And everything is clean. I hired a service as part of being the executor. The house has been cleaned once a week ever since…well, it's clean."

"Thank you, Mr. Johnson." Amber clutched the keys in her hand. "For everything."

He cleared his throat, looking embarrassed

at her thanks. "It's nothing. And I can't remember you ever calling me by my last name in the past. No sense in starting now."

She gave him a small smile. "Buddy. Thanks."

He nodded and grabbed a backpack from a rack close by. "The only thing I didn't see to before you got here was checking on the old generator up at the house. The propane tank should be full, but I haven't cleaned or tested the generator this season. There's a bad storm moving in. You might want to fire the thing up and make sure it's in good order. I'll just get you a few more things to take, to make sure you have everything that you might need." He headed around the store, loading up the backpack with more items, and sent them on their way.

The limo headed out of Mystic Glades up a long, dirt road. The "few miles" from town turned into six before they reached the house, which was unlike any mansion Dex had ever seen. It was a two-story wooden structure that reminded him more of an old farmhouse than anything else, except that it had a wing on each end that seemed to go on forever back into the trees. There was nothing remotely fancy about the outside, but he could see the locals might think of it as a mansion simply for its size.

"It's certainly…big," he offered, as he held the car door open for Amber.

A whimsical smile curved her lips. "I think Granddaddy always hoped for a large family of kids and grandkids to fill these walls one day. But it didn't exactly turn out that way."

"Why not?"

She shrugged. "He was a bit…crotchety, I suppose. A lovable heart that didn't always show on the outside unless you took the time to really get to know him."

"Thus him and Freddie not being close?"

"Right. And Freddie never married anyway, so no grandkids there. He had three sons and two daughters, but they all left Mystic Glades as soon as they could. Everyone in his family left, in one way or another."

"Except you."

"Except me." She glanced up at him. "Are we going to stand out here in the rain all day?"

He blinked and realized she was right. The fat raindrops from earlier were starting to plop down more consistently, threatening a deluge soon. He waved to the porch as the limo driver handed him the briefcase that his lawyer had gotten for him before they'd left the police station, along with the small suitcase his assistant had sent along when Dex was at Freddie's.

By the time they'd made it to the porch and

the limo was heading down the road back to Naples, the threatening rain was starting to come down in heavy sheets, turning the drive in front of the house into a big puddle.

"Ready?" Dex asked, as he set the backpack just inside the open front door along with the briefcase and suitcase.

She straightened her shoulders, facing down the dark entrance like a soldier about to go into battle. "Ready."

Chapter Seven

Amber stood in the massive, two-story entry-way, frozen in place. A warm hand touched her shoulder and she turned to see Dex standing beside her, his usual smile firmly in place.

"Good memories? Or bad?"

"Good. Mostly. Except for, well, that last day."

He hiked the backpack onto his shoulder and managed to tuck the briefcase under the same arm that was holding the suitcase. She tried to at least take the briefcase to help, but he declined.

"They say the only way to get over a bad experience is to face it head-on," he said.

"Do they? Who are they?"

"Hmm. I'm not sure. But it seems like good advice."

"Maybe. I guess I'm not used to doing that exactly. But unless you're going to turn your back and let me take off—"

"I'm not. You're stuck with me, at least until the results of the autopsy come back."

"I can't imagine that will make a difference."

"Then you're not thinking positive thoughts like you should be."

"Well, I never said I was an optimist."

"Pity. We optimists have much more fun. Speaking of fun, are the bedrooms upstairs?" He winked, making her face flush hot as he grabbed her hand in his free hand and pulled her toward the stairs.

She tugged her hand out of his grasp and took the lead. "You really need to stop trying to tow me around all of the time. I can walk perfectly fine without you pulling me along."

His hand settled onto the small of her back, sending all kinds of pleasant sensations skittering up her spine.

"Just looking after my investment," he said. "I'd hate to lose my bail bond deposit if you scamper off somewhere."

She reached the top of the stairs and turned right. "Exactly how much did you have to put down?"

"A hundred thousand dollars."

She jerked to a halt and turned around. He dropped the suitcase and briefcase and grabbed her shoulders to keep from running into her.

"A little warning might be nice next time," he muttered as he dropped his hands.

"A hundred thousand dollars?" she squeaked. "Are you crazy?"

"According to my last girlfriend, probably." He grinned.

"Stop it. Stop with the charming stuff. This is serious."

His smile faded. "Okay. Serious. Would I have survived the night in the swamp if you hadn't put that poultice on my leg to draw out the poison?"

"Um, maybe. Maybe not."

"According to the doctor your aunt brought in to see me, the answer is a definite no. You saved my life, Amber. Anything I can do to help you is the least that I can do to try to repay you. So stop worrying about me."

"But, a hundred grand. I could never repay that much."

He cocked a brow. "And you won't have to, as long as you don't take off. I won't lose more than the bail bondsman's fees unless you intend to disappear and not show up in court for your hearing whenever the date is set. You aren't, are you? Planning to take off and make me lose all that money?"

Her shoulders slumped and she turned around, leading the way down the hallway again. "Not anymore," she grumbled beneath her breath. He coughed behind her, sounding suspiciously as if he was hiding a laugh.

She stopped at the first door on the right and opened it. "There are a ridiculous number of bedrooms down both of the side wings, but this is my favorite guest—" He set everything down and continued along the hall past her. "Wait, Dex, where are you going?"

She hurried after him, catching up to him five doors down. When she saw the police crime scene tape and seal on the door, she felt the blood rush from her head.

"This is your grandfather's room?" Dex asked.

"It was. Yes."

"It's still sealed." His voice sounded incredulous.

She shrugged. "I guess so. I certainly had no reason to go back inside it. And Buddy must have told the maid service to leave it alone."

He grabbed her shoulders. "Do you realize what this means?"

"Um, that you don't get to stay in the master suite?"

He rolled his eyes. "It's a fresh crime scene, even though it's two years old. We can get some investigators out here and if they find anything to help prove your innocence it will still be admissible in court. Because nothing has been touched. The police seal on the door is proof of that."

She stared at the tape and official notice with renewed interest. "You really think there's a chance they can explain Granddaddy's death some other way?"

"The current theory is that you killed him by putting peanut oil in his tonic. Did you do that?"

"Not on purpose, no."

"Do you even remember having any peanut oil anywhere?"

"Well, no, but the coroner said it would have taken only a small amount. What if I had some peanut butter left on my hands from lunch or something and when I fixed his tonic I accidentally got some in the glass?"

"Did you have a peanut butter sandwich that day?"

"It was a long time ago."

"According to the police report, when you were interviewed the morning your grandfather was found, you said you had a turkey sandwich for lunch. Your memory would have been a lot more fresh back then. So I think it's safe to say you did not have peanut butter on your hands. Plus, you knew he was allergic, so you wouldn't have taken chances if you had. You would have washed your hands."

She pushed his hands off her shoulders and faced him with her hands on her hips. "Look, I appreciate what you're trying to do. But I racked my brain after Granddaddy died. I stepped through everything I'd done that day, over and over, trying to figure out how peanut oil could have ended up in his tonic. I couldn't figure out any way for it to happen. Do I wish I could point the finger at someone else and say they were here and they're the ones to put that in his drink? Of course I do. I wish I could say I saw someone outside, or heard a door slam, or saw someone running away. But I can't. Because I didn't see anything like that. It was raining, much like it is now. No one would have come all the way out here in that kind of weather, even if they did want to hurt Granddaddy."

"Why are you so determined to take the fall for this when you obviously didn't do it?"

"Because it's my fault." She clenched her fists beside her. "He was a sick old man with just a few months to live and all I had to do was take care of him for a little while. He trusted me, relied on me, and I let him down."

"Wait, what do you mean he only had a few months to live?"

"He had bone cancer, and it had spread all over his body. There was nothing else the doctors could do for him."

"Well, that pretty much destroys the police motive that you killed your grandfather for the money. All you had to do was wait two months and it would have all been yours. Amber, the more I hear about this, the more I think the only reason you're facing these charges today is because you ran. Running implies guilt. Why did you run?"

"Your room is this way." She turned around and headed back to the first guest room. "I'll be across the hall." She didn't wait for him to catch up to her. She headed into her old bedroom and shut and locked the door behind her.

DEX STOOD IN the hall, his hands on his hips as he stared at Amber's closed door. Something wasn't right, but damned if he could put his finger on it. Everything he'd learned about Amber Callahan in the past twenty-four hours told him she was a good person, that she cared far more about others than herself—a very rare trait that was incredibly refreshing to him after the users he met and worked with every day. Most of the people he knew wanted him for his money and power. But here he was offering Amber all of that, trying to help her, and she was instead doing everything she could to avoid his help.

Yes, she'd agreed to let him put up the bail money, but only because she hadn't realized how much. Based on her reaction a few minutes ago, he had no doubt that she'd have refused his help and stayed in jail had she realized he'd put up a hundred grand to get her out. But even after she'd grudgingly agreed to let him help her, later in the limo she'd been far more interested in trying to convince him to hire a bodyguard and worried about his safety more than hers. The only thing that had made her drop that line of conversation was when he'd promised that he would indeed get his lawyer to interview and hire a bodyguard service in the next few days.

Which brought him back to her story about the peanut oil. A woman as intelligent and caring about others as Amber obviously was wouldn't risk even having something in the house that might harm her grandfather. In fact, Dex was willing to bet his entire fortune that she'd never brought a jar of peanut butter or so much as a Snickers bar into this house. She just wouldn't risk her grandfather's life that way.

Then why was she so intent on letting people think that she was the one who'd killed her grandfather, even if it was just a mistake?

There was only one reason that Dex could think of that made sense, given what he knew about Amber.

She was protecting someone else.

AMBER STOOD IN front of the bathroom mirror, eyeing her baggy clothes with distaste. She'd obviously lost ten or fifteen pounds since she'd begun her nomad-style life, because none of her old clothes fit. Well, at least they were clean. She'd have much rather gone back to her little hut and grabbed some of her clothes that she'd bartered in exchange for a few odd jobs here and there at the Miccosukee Indian reservation. But she wasn't going anywhere without Dex, not if it could cost him a hundred thousand dollars.

She grimaced at the amount. Even if she worked two full-time jobs at the reservation, she'd never earn enough to pay him back that kind of cash. Assuming she didn't end up in prison in the first place.

She sighed and tightened her belt another notch to make sure the jeans didn't fall to her knees, then headed into the bedroom and out into the hall. The rain had stopped and the sun was going down. She hadn't eaten all day and her growling stomach was reminding her every few minutes. It was time to see what Buddy had stocked, and fix something for Dex, too. He had to be just as hungry as she was, unless he'd gone downstairs and grabbed himself something to eat while she'd been hiding out in her room for the past few hours.

His door was closed, so she knocked. "Dex?" No answer. She knocked again, then decided he must have taken a nap, so she went down the stairs, automatically avoiding the right side of the third stair from the top out of habit. It had always squeaked, and she didn't want to wake Dex with the noise. He'd been through a lot in the past few days and probably still needed extra sleep for his body to fully recover.

Most of the house was filling with shadows as the sun's last rays disappeared from the windows. But she didn't need lights to find her way through the warren of rooms. Granddaddy's eccentricities had guided all the home's rather unique additions, which often meant a wall was right where you'd least expect it, and a door might end up leading nowhere. She'd loved learning all the newest quirks of the maze of rooms and false walls with hidden staircases and hallways every summer when her parents had dropped her off to spend the time between school classes with her grandpa. Sometimes she'd wondered whether he'd designed the house the way he had just to make her laugh.

The thought of her parents squelched any urge to laugh, as it always did. She pushed thoughts of them away and finally—after going through the front entryway and a maze of smaller rooms—she arrived in the kitchen. It was about a third of the way down the west wing and was the only truly modern part of the whole house. She loved to cook, and the summer after her grandpa found that out, she'd arrived to find an ultramodern kitchen that would have made even a decent-sized restaurant groan with envy. Of course, it had been a waste on just her and her grandfather. But she'd whipped up all kinds of exotic meals to try to justify the expense of the kitchen, and to see the way his eyes closed in bliss when he tried any of her new recipes. Even the meal disasters were appreciated by her grandfather as he pretended to enjoy them.

She made her way around the marble-topped island in the middle of the expansive room and checked out the Sub-Zero refrigerator. True to his word, Buddy had fully stocked it. And like her grandfather used to do, he'd gone over-board—loading up enough food to keep her eating for months except for perishables like milk that would have to be replenished. The deep freeze on the other side of the kitchen was loaded with all kinds of meats and desserts. And the pantry, which was hidden behind a wall of what appeared to be ordinary cabinets but was actually an enormous door, contained every spice and raw ingredient her chef's heart could possibly desire.

This was one of the few material things she'd truly missed after making her decision to leave two years ago. Cooking in a real kitchen, creating culinary masterpieces, was something that made her happy like nothing else—except for seeing her grandfather's smile, of course.

She sighed and reached down to grab a couple of Delmonico steaks from one of the freezer racks.

"That sigh could fell a tree."

She jumped, bumping her head against the top of the freezer. She turned with the steaks in hand to see Dex standing near the door that led to the backyard and the vegetable garden she used to tend so long ago. The mud streaked on the bottom of the jeans he was now wearing, plus the shoeless socks peeking out from beneath them, told her he'd been outside even if he wasn't standing by the door. At least he'd had the sense to leave his muddy shoes by the door, on the little mat.

"Sorry," he said.

She closed the freezer and arched a brow in question.

"About you bumping your head," he said. "Didn't mean to startle you."

"No harm done." She started across the room, then stopped. "You're not a vegetarian, are you?"

"Definitely a meatatarian. Especially if those are steaks."

"They are."

"Yum." He headed to the sink.

"What are you doing?" She placed the steaks in the microwave to thaw them out.

"Helping. What do you want me to do? Put some potatoes in the oven to bake? Or cut them up to fry?" He washed his hands under the faucet.

"Either, I guess. Whatever you want."

"Baked sounds good." He dried his hands on the kitchen towel. "Point me to the veggies."

She laughed, both surprised and delighted that he was going to cook with her. "Over there, to the right of the freezer. Pull the door on the third cabinet in the middle."

When he did, and the entire wall opened up, he arched his brows. "Cool. Are there other surprises like this around here?"

"Everywhere."

"Tour?" he asked, looking as excited as a little boy.

"After we eat. Absolutely."

"I'll eat fast."

She shook her head at his enthusiasm and set the now defrosted steaks onto a plate to rub seasoning on them. The process of cooking, eating and then cleaning the kitchen, all the while listening to Dex talk about his time as a navy pilot and then later his adventures starting what became a billion-dollar corporation, relaxed her far more than she'd been in ages. He was an engaging speaker and made even the most mundane topics sound interesting. Just watching his eyes light up when he threw around financial investment terms she'd never much paid attention to in the past was pure joy.

She dried her hands on the kitchen towel and tossed it to him to do the same.

"And then you decided to go into business with my friend Faye's husband and become a private investigator?"

He hung the towel over the faucet to dry. "Jake was more the private investigator, because he was a former police detective when he lived in Saint Augustine."

"Where you live."

He nodded. "Faye was the target of our first case actually. She was suspected of murder."

"You're kidding."

"Don't worry. Things worked out. She was innocent—Jake proved it."

"With your help."

"Some. I can't take much credit. He's the one with the investigative skills."

"Somehow I doubt that. Or at least, I can't imagine you trying something without becoming pretty adept at it. You don't know how to fail."

"Trust me. I've been known to fail a time or two." His eyes darkened and it seemed that a shadow passed over his eyes. But then, he smiled again and seemed to shake himself out of whatever memories had bothered him. "I'm pretty sure you mentioned something about a tour earlier."

"I'm pretty sure you're right. Come on. I'll show you the general layout of the house for starters." She glanced at his socks. "Although, you might want to take those off or you'll be sliding all over the hardwood floors. The only place with carpeting is the bedrooms."

He tugged off his socks and shoved them in the pockets of his jeans. "Ready."

She took him through the west wing first, then the east wing, before finally making it upstairs nearly an hour later. He leaned against the banister, then jumped back when it wobbled.

"Whoa. That needs some tightening," he said.

She frowned in surprise. "Granddaddy was meticulous about keeping this place well repaired. I don't know why the banister would be loose like that."

"It has been two years. Maybe Buddy wasn't as worried about home maintenance as your grandfather. Do you have any tools around here? I can hammer a few nails into the base to temporarily stabilize it until we can get someone out here to do it the right way."

"Are you sure?"

He wobbled the banister again. "Positive. This is dangerous. I wouldn't want you to grab it to save yourself from a fall and have the whole thing come loose."

"All right. There's a maintenance shed out back. That's where Grandpa kept everything when I lived here. I assume the tools are still there, though he didn't use them much himself in the last few years that he was alive. He'd really slowed down by then."

"From the cancer or age?"

"Age at first, then cancer."

They went to the kitchen and he pulled his

socks and shoes on before holding the door open for her.

A shadow moved by a stand of trees twenty feet away and hurried around the back of the very building that Amber had been about to take Dex to.

"What the...? Stay here." Dex shoved her back inside and slammed the door. Then he took off running toward the building.

DEX FLATTENED HIMSELF against the side of the building and eased toward the next corner. He'd already searched the inside and made a full circuit around the outside and decided the intruder had gotten away. He was about to head back to the house when he heard a muffled sound and turned back toward the building again.

A few more feet, closer, closer. He turned the corner. Moonlight glinted off a gun. He grabbed for it and tackled the intruder to the ground, twisting the gun away from them then pressing it against their forehead.

Amber's hazel eyes stared back at him in shock.

He cursed and jerked the gun away from her, pointing down at the ground.

"What the hell are you doing out here? With a gun, no less?"

Her brows lowered. "What were you doing out here without a gun? You could have been hurt."

"And I could have shot you just now with your own gun."

She swallowed hard. "Well, yes, there is that."

He swore again and pulled her to her feet, then shoved the pistol into his waistband. He looked around to make sure that whoever he'd seen wasn't sneaking up on them, then put his hand on the small of her back because he remembered how she hated him grabbing her hand and pulling her after him.

"Come on," he urged. "Let's get inside before whoever was out here decides to come back."

Once they were inside the kitchen, he turned the lock on the door and yanked out his cell phone.

"What are you doing?" she asked.

"Calling Deputy Holder. Assuming I can get cell coverage."

She shrank away from him. "If you're worried about the gun, it belonged to my grandfather. It's registered."

"I'm not worried about the gun. I'm worried about whoever we saw skulking around the property. With you and me both outside looking for him, there was no one watching the unlocked kitchen door."

Her eyes widened and she turned around, looking at the dark opening that led into the next room before backing up against the wall beside Dex. "You think he's inside?" she whispered.

"I have no idea. But I'm not about to take any chances." When Holder came on the phone, Dex told him about the shadowy figure he'd seen behind the house. After ending the call, he pulled the gun out of his waistband. "Let's sit at the kitchen table until Holder gets here with some deputies to help search the house."

She sat beside him while he aimed the pistol at the doorway.

"Why didn't you tell Holder about the gun?" she asked.

"Because before he gets here, we're hiding the gun. He doesn't need to know it even exists."

"Why?"

He glanced down at her before looking back at the opening. "Because I'm pretty sure someone out on bond for a murder charge isn't supposed to have any weapons. They could yank your bail and lock you right back up."

She shivered beside him. "I hadn't thought of that. Thank you."

"It's my job to think of things like that."

"Your job?"

"You know...as a deputy and all." He grinned.

She rolled her eyes.

"Where was the gun hidden anyway?" he asked.

She waved vaguely toward the far wall. "In a hidden panel."

"How many of these hidden panels are there?"

"Too many to count."

"Do they all contain guns?"

"Of course not. Just the ones by the front door, the back door here, and in Grandpa's bedroom upstairs."

He shook his head.

"What?" she asked. "Why does that seem to worry you?"

"Well, let me see. The house has been vacant for two years. And someone was skulking around the property like they know it really well and managed to slip past me even though I was out there trying to find them. I have to think they know this place, and if they've been slipping in and out of the house for the past few years, they might know all of the hiding places, too."

"Meaning they could have one of Grandpa's guns."

"Yep. And Holder's a good hour outside Mystic Glades. I'm thinking we might want to hunker down somewhere more defensible than this kitchen while we wait for backup."

"I couldn't agree more."

"Is there a room without any windows close by?"

"The pantry, I guess?"

"That works." They headed toward the wall of cabinets.

A distant squeak sounded from somewhere deep in the house. They both froze.

"Any idea what that was?" Dex asked.

"Yes. It was the stairs," she whispered. "Someone's inside the house."

Dex hurried to the cabinets and yanked the door open. "Get in."

She went inside but stopped and turned around when he didn't join her. "What are you doing? Come in here with me."

He shoved the gun into her hands. "Barricade the door and don't let anyone in but me or Deputy Holder."

"Wait," she whispered harshly. "Dex, you're not going out there without the gun. And I'm not hiding in here while you're risking your life."

He leaned down and tilted her chin up. "Amber, there's no way in hell you're going with me. And I'm not leaving you here defenseless. Take the gun, and barricade the door."

He gently shoved her back and pulled the door closed.

Amber gritted her teeth and yanked the door open.

But Dex was gone, and the lights were off.

Chapter Eight

Dex crouched against the wall, keeping as still as possible as he peered down the second-floor hallway in the east wing. Unless he remembered incorrectly, there were no balconies off this section of the house. Which meant whoever he'd followed up here was trapped. And that made him dangerous.

There. A dull thump, from one of the rooms on the right. He inched his way down the hall and stopped in front of the door that seemed the most likely to be where the intruder was hiding. A second later, another thump.

Dex carefully turned the doorknob, then threw the door open and ran inside. He saw the silhouette of someone by the window, but he knew that silhouette now.

"Damn it, Amber. How did you even get up here?"

The light flicked on overhead. Amber stood a few feet away, the pistol wedged in her waistband. "I wasn't about to cower in the pantry while you went off after an intruder. Especially since you left the gun with me."

"Did it occur to you that I'm trying to protect you?"

"Yes. And I appreciate it. But welcome to the modern age. I can protect myself."

He sighed. "I suppose you can. But that doesn't mean I'm not going to try to protect you anyway. I'm clinging to my Neanderthal roots."

She laughed.

He grinned. "You should do that more." His grin faded and he turned around. "Since I don't see anyone else up here, I'm guessing the bad guy got away before I made it upstairs. How did you get up here without passing me?"

"I used the back stairs."

"Back stairs? Where?"

She stepped to the wall and pressed a decal of a flower. A panel slid back to reveal a dark hole. Dex peeked into the opening.

"I should have expected something like that in a house like this. You left this off the tour."

"Yeah, well, I hadn't intended to show it to you, to be honest." At his questioning glance, she added, "But that was before I learned about the exorbitant fortune you put down to bail me out. I guess I can show you the rest of the house and all of its secrets now that I'm not going to run away again."

He eyed the opening. "If I came up the main stairs, and you came up these back stairs, where did the intruder go?"

"Like you said, he had to have gotten downstairs before you made it from the kitchen to the second floor."

"I'm not liking this at all. He could be anywhere. This house is way too big to secure. I think we should move back to your aunt's bar until this is over. At least there I knew where the exits were and there weren't any hidden panels or staircases to worry about."

Amber bit her bottom lip and looked away.

Dex blinked at her. "There are hidden panels and staircases at Freddie's?"

She nodded. "A couple. Honestly, they're all over this town. My grandfather was a bit... eccentric. And he founded Mystic Glades. He pretty much left his stamp on everything."

"So, who all knows about these hidden passageways?"

"Everyone, I guess."

"Even in this house?"

She shrugged. "I suppose not. I mean, people are bound to assume that there are hidden passageways. But unless Grandpa or I took them on a tour, they wouldn't know where the openings are or what to look for."

"Can you think of anyone besides you, and his children obviously, who might know?"

Her look turned guarded, and he immediately knew she was hiding something. Again. The only question was why.

"Not really," she said. "Grandpa wasn't big on socializing and I certainly never had anyone over."

He waited, hoping she'd level with him, but when she didn't say anything else, he swallowed his disappointment. "Okay. Then we're back to assuming no one knows about the hidden areas. So as long as Holder helps us search the house to insure no one's still inside hiding somewhere, we should be okay."

"Agreed."

He moved toward the door. "We might as well go downstairs and wait for Holder below. We can set up a defensible position in the main living room in the front, with our backs to the fireplace."

"You're not going to try to make me hide in a closet?"

He rolled his eyes. "I've given up on trying to make you do anything."

Half an hour later, red-and-blue flashing lights lit up the windows on the front room. Per their agreement, Amber hid the gun in a wall panel before Dex answered the door. Holder stood on the porch with three other deputies. The lines at the corners of his eyes were tense and his right hand hovered near the pistol on his belt.

"Bring me up to speed," he said.

A few minutes later, two of the deputies were searching the property in the back where Amber and Dex had seen someone skulking by the maintenance building, while the third deputy stayed with Holder inside the house. They made a circuit of the entire house, one with Amber and one with Dex so they could show them through the maze of rooms. By the time they were done, Dex was convinced no one was in the house, and that no one had probably ever been inside, because the only footprints they saw were those of Dex and Amber.

"The noise we heard on the stairs earlier must have been the house settling," Dex said.

Amber didn't look convinced, but she nodded anyway.

"Well, everything's locked up safe and sound now," Holder said. "We did find footprints in the backyard that don't match either of your shoes. So there was definitely someone out there. Probably just some neighborhood kid curious about someone being at the Callahan mansion since it's been vacant for so long. Whoever they were, they're long gone now." He arched a brow. "If you're worried about staying out here alone, I can take you back to Naples with me. You can set up in a hotel."

Dex looked at Amber. "It's up to you."

She immediately shook her head. "I'd rather stay here, if it's all the same to you."

"We'll stay."

"Suit yourself," Holder said. "Oh, since I'm out here, I might as well update you about the case, Miss Callahan. Your grandfather's body has been exhumed and the private coroner that Mr. Lassiter hired will begin the autopsy in the morning."

"So soon?" she said.

He slanted a glance at Dex. "Money is known for making things happen. I reckon you'll have results later tomorrow, if not sooner."

"Thank you," Amber said, her voice small.

Holder nodded. "Call us if you need us, but remember we're an hour out. So if something happens again you might want to seriously consider getting someone to bring you back to town." He cocked a brow at Dex. "Unless you've decided to give up your glamorous new role as a cop and want to turn Miss Callahan over to me to take back to jail."

"And give up my shiny gold star?" He rubbed his shirt as if he really did have a star on it. "I don't think so."

Holder shook his head and herded his men out of the house. After the police cars were heading down the driveway, Dex closed and locked the door. Amber stood silently staring at the floor.

"Amber, you okay?"

She looked up and shrugged. "It just seems so…wrong…to dig up my grandfather's body. We already know how he died."

He put his hands on her shoulders. "I don't think he'd mind us disturbing his grave if it means we might find something to help prove your innocence."

Her gaze didn't meet his as she nodded, which only reinforced his earlier suspicion that she was hiding something.

"If there was something about your grandfather's death that you haven't told anyone, you'd tell now, wouldn't you? Knowing it could mean the difference between prison and freedom? And remember that Florida is a capital-punishment state. The prosecutor could go for the death penalty."

She shivered and rubbed her hands up and down her arms. "I know. I'm tired. I think I'll head on up to bed." Without another word, she headed up the stairs and disappeared into her room.

Dex sighed, retrieved the gun from the panel in the family room and then headed up to his room.

AMBER LAY IN bed staring at the ceiling. She couldn't sleep, not with so many worries on her mind. Who was the intruder who'd been in the backyard? What did he want? Was it really just a teenager—or someone more sinister?

And what, if anything, should she do about telling the truth about what happened to her grandfather?

Years ago she'd made a decision that she'd wondered many times about later on. But after coming back to Mystic Glades, she'd seen the reason for her lies and felt the same surge of protectiveness that she had before she'd left. What she was doing made sense because she knew it was what her grandfather would want. And it had never hurt before, until she'd met Dex. Now she was feeling things she hadn't felt since she was in high school: that delicious rush of heat every time she looked at him, the pleasant tightening of her belly when she'd seen him without his shirt, the tingle of anticipation when he held her hand. She had a crush on Dex Lassiter. There was no denying it. Except that this crush was far worse than any she'd ever experienced before. She couldn't stop thinking about him or seeing his face whenever he wasn't around. And it was because of these overwhelming feelings that she was in the trouble she was in right now. If she hadn't been so eager to see him again, and so driven to make sure that he was okay, she'd be home right now, "home" being her place in the Glades instead of this monstrosity that she still thought of as her grandfather's house.

It wasn't her home. Not really. It was her sanctuary and refuge when her parents had left her here each summer, a way to escape the constant bickering and fighting and tension in her house between two people who supposedly had loved each other once, a very long time ago. Her grandfather had been very private and pretty much regarded as the town scrooge, but he'd seen through her pain as a teenager and had rather forcefully insisted that her parents go off on an extended vacation in Europe the summer of her junior year. The fact that he'd dumped a boatload of money on them to sweeten the pot had worked and they'd jetted off for a vacation. And Amber had spent that first, awkward summer with her grandfather, feeling abandoned and unloved. Until she got to know him. And then she saw the marshmal-

low inside him and knew he loved her deeply
and that he'd been trying to save her, in his
own way.

From then on out they'd become each other's champions, existing in a usually quiet but
comfortable camaraderie with each other. And
when her parents ended up staying in Europe
after her graduation, she knew her grandfather was behind that, that he must have made
it a financial windfall for them to stay away.
She'd gone to college and spent all her breaks
with her grandfather, and had mostly done the
same thing that her parents had done to her—
she'd forgotten about them. Until her grandfather's death, when they'd returned just long
enough to find out that they weren't mentioned
in his will. Then they'd done what they were
so good at—they'd disappeared, without hanging around long enough to see what had happened to Amber.

She shoved the covers back and slid out of
bed. Enough of this. She was making herself
miserable thinking about the past, about the
only people in her life she should have been
able to count on and rely on who'd never, not
once, been there for her.

A board creaked in the hallway outside her
bedroom. She froze and looked around for
some kind of weapon, but Dex had taken her

gun. She grabbed a heavy bookend from a bookshelf by the bed and tiptoed to the door. Then she quietly, carefully, turned the knob and yanked the door open.

Dex swore and grabbed the bookend out of her raised hand. "Good grief, Amber. What are you doing with that?"

"I heard a noise."

He grimaced and stepped to his left, making a board squeak. "Was that what you heard?"

"Yes. What are you doing outside my door?"

"I was pacing the hall. Couldn't sleep. But as soon as I stepped on that board I was worried you might have heard it and might be scared. I was waiting to see if I'd woken you so I could reassure you that the noise was just me."

"Oh." She felt her face flush hot. "I wasn't scared."

He set the bookend on a decorative table against the wall. "Of course not." He winked. "Well, sorry again for waking you. I'll just… go back to my room."

"Okay. Night."

"Night." He hesitated, his gaze dropping to the nightshirt that barely came to the tops of her thighs before he seemed to wrench his gaze away. He cleared his throat. "See you in the morning."

She watched in silence as he went into his

room across the hall and shut the door. The heat in his gaze was unmistakable and had sparked an answering tug in her belly. And suddenly she was thinking things she shouldn't be thinking. Because having a crush was one thing. But taking it to the next level, to a level where there was no coming back from, was quite another. She shouldn't be thinking about holding him close, about running her fingers over his rippling muscles. About seeing if he kissed as good when he was conscious as he had when he'd been burning up with fever back by the spring.

No, it was wrong to think about being with him, even if he wanted her as much as she wanted him. Because there was no future, no possibility of one, while she was wanted for murder and had no way to prove she hadn't done it without destroying someone else. Lying, even though she hated it, was accomplishing the only good thing she'd ever done in her life. If protecting her grandfather's best friend from the horrible mistake that he'd made meant sacrificing herself, it was a price she was willing to pay. Because it was the only way she could repay her grandfather for being the only person who'd ever really cared about her. And she never wanted to be the selfish, self-centered type of person that both of her parents had been. Living a life like that was no life and wasn't a future she was willing to contemplate. She'd rather have no future and die knowing that she'd done the right thing.

She started to step back and close the door, but she stopped and stared longingly at the closed door across the hall. She'd had so little love in her life, and only one disastrous intimate relationship in college with a guy who'd ended up more concerned with notches on his bedpost than the lasting relationship she'd hoped to have. So how could she even consider what amounted to a one-night stand with Dex? She barely knew him.

But she already knew he was worlds better than the immature boy from her past.

Dex was all man—tall, strong, incredibly appealing in every way. And he had that sexy smile that made her want to grab him and kiss him every time he aimed it her way. But he was so much more than that, just based on what he'd said when he'd been delirious. She knew that he'd been worried about leaving his company to fly out to Mystic Glades, but he'd done it anyway because he wanted to protect his best friend from what Dex believed might be a very bad decision. And as soon as he'd realized his friend Jake had thought it all through and was determined to continue on the route he'd chosen, Dex had supported him in that decision.

And then when he'd found himself here, even knowing that someone was trying to kill him, he'd continued to put his life on hold to help her, a stranger, simply because he felt an obligation to her for helping him after the crash. He was putting all his resources behind trying to help her. And then he'd risked his life for her twice tonight—first going after the intruder by the shed and then going through the house in the dark, without a weapon, to find the intruder because they'd both believed him to be inside. What did she know about Dex? She knew that he was a good person, kind, and genuinely caring.

She curled her fingers around the doorjamb. If loving him, just this once, was a mistake, why did the thought of being in his arms feel so right? She was tired, so tired, of being on guard and worrying all the time. Just this once, she wanted to push all her worries aside and simply live. Especially if she'd be spending the rest of her life in prison or—worse—facing the death penalty.

With that thought, she pushed herself forward until she was standing at Dex's door. This was what she wanted, one night of joy, one night to treasure and hold close to get her through the darkness that surely lay ahead.

She turned the knob, then slowly pushed the door open. "Dex?" she whispered. If he was asleep, she'd go back to her room and know that this was a mistake.

The covers rustled in the big four-poster bed. "Amber? What's wrong?" He slid out of bed, the moonlight glinting through a slit in the curtains, revealing that he was wearing only boxers.

Her mouth went dry at the sight of all that skin and those sculpted muscles as he strode toward her. He stopped in front of her and moved her to the side as he peered into the hallway. Always the protector. She loved that about him, even though she knew she could protect herself.

"Nothing's wrong," she said.

He stepped back and turned around. "Then why—"

She pushed the door closed and, for emphasis, turned the lock. "I don't want to be alone tonight."

His Adam's apple bobbed in his throat and his hand shook as he swept her hair back from her face. "Canoe Girl, don't tempt me. Because since I met you, I've been thinking about little else but getting you into bed." He dropped his hands to his sides, his fingers curling into fists as if to make him stop from reaching for her.

"Why fight it, then? I want the same thing." She reached for her nightshirt to take it off, but he grabbed her wrists.

"Don't. I'm trying to be noble here. You're just feeling beholden to me because I paid your bail and hired a lawyer. I wouldn't want you to feel obligated. Please, go back to your room." He reached for the doorknob, but she moved in front of him.

"Amber—"

"Dex," she whispered back, as she swiftly pulled her nightshirt over her head and tossed it to the floor.

His eyes widened and his mouth dropped open as he looked his fill. She was completely naked and knew she was being unfair. But just the fact that he was trying to be noble had made her want him even more. He truly was a good guy. She just wished she'd met him years ago, that he could have been her first, and maybe her last, and that she could have been anywhere but here back when her grandfather had gotten sick. Maybe, just maybe, things would have turned out differently.

She ruthlessly stepped forward, sliding her hands up his glorious chest, reveling in the catch in his breath and how his muscles tensed beneath her fingertips. She slid her fingers up, up, up until her body was pressed flush against his and her hands were behind his neck. A shudder racked his entire body, and he groaned. It was a groan of surrender, because suddenly he was pulling her tighter against him, against the hardening erection pulsing against her belly, and molding his lips to hers.

His kiss was like fire, igniting all her nerve endings, tightening her belly almost painfully and melting her insides. She shifted against him, their mouths greedily moving against each other as she tried to get closer, closer. He reached down and lifted her into his arms, one arm beneath her bottom, his hand molded against her thigh as the other wrapped around her back. He turned with her in his arms and pressed her against the door.

His tongue dueled with hers, tasting, teasing, fanning her pleasure higher and higher. He broke the kiss, both of them gasping for air as he moved his mouth to the side of her neck. She leaned her head sideways, shivering in delight at the feel of his lips, his tongue, against the sensitive skin of her collarbone.

Unable to bear the growing pressure inside her, she rubbed her body against his and angled one arm down his back to his hip. He jerked against her, the cloth of his underwear the only barrier keeping him from penetrating her. He shuddered again and moved back to her mouth. But, instead of kissing her, he stared down into her eyes.

"Are you sure about this?" he whispered.

In answer she stroked her hand down his flank.

He growled low in his throat and captured her lips in a searing kiss as he turned and stumbled toward the bed. Holding her with his hand beneath her bottom, he used his other hand to rake the covers back, then gently laid her down on the soft mattress. But, instead of following her down, he pressed a quick, hard kiss against her lips and let her go.

"Dex—"

"I'll be right back."

She turned her head on the pillow and watched him cross the room to the dresser. His suitcase was sitting open on top. He fumbled inside and when he turned around she realized what he was holding. A condom. Or, more accurately, a box of them. He tore the top off, grabbed one and let the box drop to the floor as he hurried back to the bed and sat down on the side of the mattress.

"You always travel with a box of condoms?" she asked.

"My assistant packed them when he sent everything to me." He hesitated, the packet in his hand. "If you want to stop, I'll understand. I'm not exactly a celibate guy or a wait-until-marriage kind of man. Some might even call me a womanizer. Obviously my assistant thinks so, since he made sure I was prepared for any… ah…emergency." He gave her a lopsided grin.

He waited, looking like he fully expected her to tell him to forget it. But just the fact that he was being honest was an added turn-on for her. Honesty was so rare, and to her knowledge Dex had never lied to her, about anything. And even though "womanizer" wasn't in the least bit flattering, he'd readily admitted that the label might fit. But did it really?

She ran a finger down his thigh, delighting in how his muscles tightened beneath her touch. "Are you one of those one-night-stand kinds of guys?"

He slowly shook his head, watching her finger as it moved toward his inner thigh. "No." His voice was raw, tight. "If this…what we're doing…is a one-night stand, then I'd have to admit it's a first for me. But I'm not one for being alone, either. I like being in a relationship." He gave her a wry smile. "I'm just not very good at them."

She stopped with her hand poised just inches

from his erection, tenting his boxers. "Are you in one now, a relationship?"

He frowned. "Of course not. I would never cheat on anyone."

She hooked her finger inside the elastic band. "Then what are we waiting for?"

His smile in the dark made him look like a charming rogue. "I have no idea." In no time he'd shucked his underwear and rolled on the condom. Then he was pressing her back against the mattress, the light matting of hair on his chest tickling her sensitive skin.

Any doubts or worries that she'd had disappeared beneath the flood of sensations he was awakening inside her. Like a master, he stroked her body like a fine instrument, stimulating every nerve ending, making her restless and yearning beneath him, never knowing where the next stroke would occur. Although he seemed to touch her everywhere, his movements were unhurried as he fully devoted himself to wringing out every last bit of pleasure that he could in one spot before moving to the next.

It was as if he wanted to leave no part of her untouched, unclaimed, before he finally moved up her body and captured her lips again. For the first time ever, she let go, allowing herself to submerge completely, awash in the flood of emotions and feelings he'd created inside her. She was just as eager as he, touching everywhere, stroking, petting, caressing until she felt she'd die from the pleasure of it.

And then he moved above her, looking deep into her eyes as he poised himself at her entrance and laced his fingers with hers above her head. He leaned down, slowly, oh so slowly, and gave her the sweetest kiss ever as he pressed inside her. It had been so long, too long, and she tensed against the invasion. But he whispered reassuring words in her ear, then made love to her mouth with his lips and tongue in rhythm to the movements of his hips, capturing her gasps of surprise and pleasure. She relaxed beneath his sensual onslaught and was soon just as frenzied as him, straining toward the next peak, riding the sensations higher and higher until an explosion of pleasure shot through her and she cried out his name.

He soon joined her in his own climax and collapsed against the mattress, rolling to his side with her in his arms.

Chapter Nine

Dex put away the last frying pan and plopped the dish towel on the countertop as he eyed Amber washing the kitchen table.

She glanced up at him, then quickly looked away, her face heating to a pretty shade of pink that wasn't actually so pretty since he knew why she was blushing. She'd barely been able to put together two words since they'd woken up in each other's arms this morning. What he didn't know yet was whether she regretted making love with him or whether she was just being shy because she was so inexperienced.

He winced. How many lovers had he had over the years? A dozen? Maybe more? And if he guessed right Amber had probably had only one lover other than him. And the only reason he figured she'd even had one was because she wasn't a virgin. He'd taken her boldness at the beginning of the evening as a sign that she was comfortable with what they were going to do, that she wanted him as much as he wanted her. Now he wasn't so sure. Regrets? Yeah, even if she didn't have any, he sure as hell did. He knew better than to take advantage of someone as innocent as her. In the light of day, knowing her future was so uncertain right now, he felt doubly like a heel, as if he'd really taken advantage of her when he should have been protecting her from the harsh world that her aunt certainly didn't care about protecting her from. Amber had no one in her corner. He should have been her champion, should have been strong enough to say no when she came to his room. He swore beneath his breath.

Amber jumped and turned, her hands clutching the damp paper towels that she'd just used to clean the table. "Something wrong?" she asked, her gaze darting to the back door as if expecting to see another intruder.

He shook his head. "No. Sorry. Just thinking." He glanced at his watch, then at the dark clouds hanging in the sky. "It's closer to lunchtime than breakfast, not that you can tell with the clouds blocking out the sun. I imagine Garreth will call soon to give us an update on the case."

She tossed the paper towels into the trash can beneath the sink and shut the cabinet. "You don't think the medical examiner would really have something to say already about my grand-father do, you? Won't he have to run tests?"

He shrugged. "Can't say for sure. I'm no expert on things like that. But I'm hopeful it won't take long." As much money as he was paying his lawyer to encourage him to speed things along any way possible, he'd be surprised if it took long at all. Garreth could work miracles, and Dex made a point of not asking how he did it. Most of his lawyer's tactics fell into a need-to-know category and Dex figured he didn't need to know. Plus, in this case, his lawyer had already told him that "samples" had been taken and preserved from the original autopsy, so the testing had begun last night courtesy of a private lab in town that had been generously encouraged to work all night. Dex was not a patient man and he had enough money that he didn't usually have to be patient.

He leaned back against the counter with his legs spread in front of him. "The investigation would probably go much faster if you admitted whatever you know about what really happened."

She met his stare, unblinking. "I've said everything that I'm going to say. There's nothing else that I can say."

"Why? Who matters to you so much that

you'd lie and risk the death penalty to protect them?"

This time it was her turn to wince. Obviously she didn't relish the idea of facing a death penalty. Maybe that was the weapon that he could use to get her to tell him the truth.

He shoved away from the sink and moved to stand directly in front of her, making her crane her neck back to meet his gaze. He was much taller than her and he wasn't above using that to his advantage, to intimidate. Usually he used his height and his brawn to intimidate men across a boardroom table or in a dinner party that was really more of a mental wrestling match to see who could gain the upper hand with a potential client for a future investment. But if using his physical size and strength to get Amber to back down would save her from prison, or worse, he was all for it.

"Tell me about that night," he said.

"I already did, and it's part of the public record that I'm sure you've already read."

"Tell me again. But this time, don't leave out the part about why you supposedly would want to kill your grandfather."

She shook her head. "I never said that I wanted to hurt my grandfather. I didn't. It was an accident."

He may have found the perfect weapon, even better than the threat of a death penalty. Amber obviously loved her grandfather very much. The idea that she'd hurt him on purpose was repugnant to her. She wouldn't want anyone else to believe that, either.

"Did he ever leave the house?"

"Once or twice a year, maybe. Other than that, he pretty much stayed on the property. He liked to work in the garden out back."

"You were in charge of the groceries, then? Buying everything for the household?"

"Yes."

"If you didn't want to hurt him, why would you buy peanuts, then, when you knew he was highly allergic?"

"I…must have made a mistake. Grabbed them by accident and tossed them in the pantry without thinking."

"Then why didn't the police find anything in the pantry?"

Her gaze dropped from his as she tried to think of something plausible, which only had Dex fisting his hands together. It was so painfully obvious that she was innocent. How could the police not have seen that years ago? He'd have to ask Holder and Garreth to review the original interview. She'd never been taken to the police station, had only been questioned at the house. So maybe that was the problem? They hadn't had the kind of in-depth questioning that might have revealed her subterfuge, and whoever had asked her questions didn't note her body language or hesitation or just plain didn't know how to read someone.

"Amber?" he prodded. "Why didn't the police find anything to do with peanuts when they searched the house?"

"Maybe I…threw it out?"

"They looked through the trash. If you're going to lie, you need to come up with something better than that."

Her face reddened. "It was a…traumatic event that morning. I wasn't thinking straight. I was more worried with trying to save Grandpa. If there weren't any peanuts or peanut oil here, then maybe one of the jars that I used to mix his tonic had been used for peanuts in the past. And I didn't wash it well enough. I don't know. All I know for sure is that no one else was here, no one else could have done it."

Again, her gaze slid away. And again, Dex knew, with absolute certainty, that she was lying.

He shoved his hands in his pockets and moved past her to look out the back windows. "You know, they say lethal injection is far more painful than people think. You don't just go to sleep and feel nothing."

"Don't you think I know that?" she snapped.

"Then tell me what happened that day."

She joined him at the window and stared out. "He was sick, with the flu or something similar. And he was miserable, achy. I wanted to take him to Naples to see a doctor, or get a doctor to come see him here, but Grandpa was...stubborn. He insisted he'd be okay and refused to see anyone. He wanted me to take care of him. And I had been doing that for a long time—always have been a healer, basically. So when he refused a doctor I went into town to get a few things I'd need in addition to the plants I grew in the garden for mixing potions. When I got back, I mixed his tonic and gave it to him. He was resting comfortably at bedtime so I went to bed without another thought about it. When I woke up, he was...gone."

"You went to town? Where? For what?"

Her shoulders tensed, and he knew she must have slipped, in telling him about going to town. Had something happened in town that made her suspect who might have something to do with her grandfather's death? And if she loved her grandfather so much, why would she protect him or her?

"I needed…supplies."

"Okay. So you went where?"

"Here and there." At his exasperated look, she said, "I'm pretty sure I went to The Moon."

"The Moon? I saw a shop across from Buddy's that was called The Moon and Star. Faye Star owns it, from what Jake told me. Is that what you're talking about?"

"Yes. It was just The Moon when I lived here. They have potions, too, and sometimes I use those as raw ingredients in the things that I mix up."

"So maybe you grabbed something with peanut oil in it on accident?"

She shook her head. "No. Impossible."

"Why do you say that?"

"Because as soon as we realized that Grandpa had most likely died of an allergic reaction, I called and asked about peanuts. The owner of The Moon at the time was also allergic to peanuts and never has them in the store, in any form. The tonic couldn't have gotten contaminated that way."

"Because you checked. Which just goes to prove that you really don't know how the peanuts ended up in there, do you? But you suspect someone else who may know, right?"

"Why do you keep saying that?"

"You have an honest face, Amber. Every

time something bothers you it shows in your eyes, in the way you tense up. And in your voice. It's like you have a light bulb on top of your head and it blinks every time you try to talk around the truth. And you've done nothing but talk around the truth every time I ask you about your grandfather's death. You're hiding something. You may not know exactly how he died, but you suspect someone. I thought you loved your grandfather?"

"I do. I did. Very much."

"Then why would you protect the one person that you think might have been responsible for his death?"

She closed her eyes as if in pain. "It's not that simple." She shoved the back door open and walked out onto the porch.

Dex followed her out, refusing to let her drop their conversation. They didn't have a lot of time, especially with Garreth pressing for answers. If those answers ended up being nothing to change things, then Amber was in a world of trouble. He had to make her see that.

"You said you loved your grandfather, and yet you're protecting someone who could very well have killed him. Explain that to me."

When she didn't say anything, he gently cupped her face. "Amber, trust me. I want to help you. But I can't, not if you don't tell me the truth." He stared down at her, waiting. "Amber, where else did you go that day? Besides The Moon?"

She stepped back, shaking her head.

A bush near the bottom of the steps rustled. Dex shoved Amber behind him just as a man stepped out from behind the shrub. Buddy Johnson. He wore the same faded jeans and red-and-black-striped shirt he'd worn yesterday at his store, but they looked rumpled, like he'd slept in them. And big bags beneath his eyes told the story of a very restless night.

"Mr. Johnson," Dex said, "What are you doing here?"

His sad eyes lifted from Amber, who had moved back beside Dex, and rose to meet Dex's gaze. "I can tell you where else she went that day, Mr. Lassiter. And I can tell you whom she's trying to protect."

"Buddy. Don't," Amber pleaded.

He gave her a sad smile. "You're a good person, Amber Callahan. And I hate to admit that I was one of the ones who thought you might have had something to do with your granddaddy's death right after it happened. But I know better now. And I know who you're trying to protect."

"Who?" Dex asked. "Who is it?"

Buddy straightened his shoulders. "Me. She's trying to protect me."

"THIS DOESN'T MAKE any sense." Dex rested his forearms on his knees as he sat forward on the couch in the living room across from Amber and Buddy on the opposite couch. "Amber, you thought Buddy was the one who killed your grandfather?"

"Accidentally. Yes."

"How?"

"I went to Buddy's store to buy a new blanket because Granddad loved those thermal ones Buddy sells and Granddad's was threadbare. Buddy is the one who packed the blanket and some other supplies into my backpack, including some new jars that I always order from him for making my tonics. Since I knew I didn't have any peanuts in the house, those jars were the only way there could have been any peanut residue. I realized that later, and I knew Buddy would never intentionally harm my grandfather. They were best friends. I figured he had to have had the jars stored with peanuts or something and didn't think about it."

"But why wouldn't you tell the police?"

She and Buddy both shared a frown, a united front, before she continued. "The police have never shown much love for Mystic

Glades residents. I didn't trust them to think it was an accident. I couldn't risk something happening to Buddy."

"But why? Why would you sacrifice yourself to protect him, especially if it was an accident?"

Buddy put his arm around her shoulders as if to protect her from Dex, which was really rather ludicrous, given the situation. "Mr. Lassiter, Amber's a good woman and I'm sure she thought I wouldn't be able to handle prison and she could. We always stand up for each other and she's always respected her elders."

Dex suspected there was more to it than that, but for now, he let it drop. "Okay, so is Amber right? That the jars you gave her were tainted?"

"I think so, yes. But I didn't realize it at the time. I thought— Well, I'm sorry, Amber, but I couldn't figure out any other way, so I assumed you'd done it."

She shrugged. "How could you not? Even my own aunt thought the same thing. Still does."

"Yes, well, it was a few weeks later that I was unpacking the rest of those jars when I realized a shipment of peanuts had come in the same box and were sitting beneath a layer of tissue paper. I figured during the shipment some of the peanuts had shifted and gotten oil on the jars. But by then, Amber was gone and there was nothing I could do to help her."

"You could have helped her yesterday, by going into town and telling the police what had happened."

He nodded. "You're right. But I was scared, and ashamed. It took me a bit of time to come to my senses. I wanted to tell her first, and I came out last night to do that very thing. But then you saw me and came after me and I ran."

"It was you out by the shed?" Dex asked.

"Yes. Like I said, I lost my nerve, so I took off. But I'm here now to tell what I know. You can call the police and I'll confess."

Dex rolled his eyes. Confess? He'd never seen two innocent people more intent on confessing to their crimes before. "Confession is for guilty people, Mr. Johnson. You didn't try to kill Mr. Callahan any more than Amber did. It was one big accident all around. I just have one more question before I call Deputy Holder. Why did you go into the house last night?"

Buddy's brows lowered. "Go into the house? I didn't. Why would you think that I did?"

Dex exchanged a look with Amber. "We heard something and thought someone was inside."

Buddy shook his head. "I didn't try to go inside. I had no reason to."

"Okay," Dex said. "Maybe there's another explanation, like the house settling. I don't know. I'll call Holder. I just wish we had some kind of proof to make the case stronger to help Amber."

"Oh, I have proof. Right here." Buddy took an envelope from the pocket of his shirt and handed it to Amber.

She opened it and pulled out two pictures. Dex got up and squatted down in front of the couch, looking at the pictures with her. They showed a box of bottles with tissue paper beneath them but flipped up at one corner to show a bag of peanuts that had a rip in it, with the peanuts all over the bottom of the box.

"That's your proof?" Dex said. "You could have taken that picture today."

"Nope. Look at the bottom right corner, the label on the box."

Amber raised the picture higher as she and Dex tried to read the date. "It's from the week when Granddaddy died," Amber said.

"It sure is. With my store's name on it. And the peanuts, you can tell, are fresh. The picture is legit."

"Okay, then, what about proof that Amber actually bought some of those bottles at your store that day?" Dex asked.

"I keep records of all of that in my logbooks. I can get them."

"No, don't bother. We'll wait until Holder gets here and then he can get them. That will be better. Speaking of which, I'll call him now."

He left Amber and Buddy holding hands and whispering to each other like long-lost friends as he stepped into one of the rooms without windows in the middle of the mazelike house just far enough away so no one could hear him. He explained to Holder exactly what he'd just been told.

"Interesting," Holder said. "That certainly makes it plausible that there was no intent to harm. And, combined with what the coroner found, I'm sure Miss Callahan is going to be quite pleased."

"What did the coroner find?"

"Mr. Callahan didn't die from an allergic reaction."

Dex's hand tightened around the phone. "You're kidding me."

"Nope. There was peanut oil in that tonic, but only faint traces, probably enough to corroborate the story that the glass was packed in a box with peanuts as opposed to someone trying to add enough oil to kill him. But when the coroner performed some tests, at your lawyer's insistence, she determined the ingredients in the tonic would have rendered any allergic types of reactions irrelevant because the tonic was a natural antihistamine. It would have counteracted anything to do with the peanut allergy even if it were triggered. Mr. Callahan's death is now being labeled as 'natural causes.'"

"Heart attack?"

"Respiratory. The cancer weakened his lungs and the flu was the final straw. He just couldn't take it. As of right this minute, all the charges against Amber Callahan are dropped."

Chapter Ten

Amber stood on the back porch, watching the play of lightning across the dark afternoon sky. Heavy rain clouds warned of another storm that would break across the Glades and probably turn the small water inlets into fast-flowing rivers for the next few days.

Dex stood beside her but, instead of watching the sky, he was watching her. "You should be happy," he said.

"I am. I guess. It's just so…surprising. Sudden."

"Sudden? You lived in exile for two years."

"I know. That's not what I mean. One day I know who I am and what I'm doing and less than a week later a plane drops out of the sky." She turned to face him. "And everything changed. Now I have a life again, a future. And I have you to thank for that." She entwined her arms around his neck and stepped into the cocoon of his arms.

He hugged her tight and rested his cheek on the top of her head. "I still don't understand. Why did you try to cover for Buddy?"

She tightened her arms around him. "You won't understand, even if I explain it."

"Try me."

She closed her eyes and rested her head against his chest. "All my life, the only person who ever cared about me—in my family, at least—was my grandfather. And my friend Faye, of course. But my grandfather was the one who was always there for me no matter what. From the time I was little until the day he died. He did everything for me. He basically saved me by bribing my self-centered parents to move away and leave me with him. He gave me security, love, financial stability, and he only asked one thing in return—that I take care of his friend, Buddy."

"What do you mean? Buddy's a grown man. He doesn't need anyone to take care of him."

She pulled back and looked at him. "Buddy doesn't need money—he's got plenty of his own because of some kind of swamp buggy invention. Grandpa just wanted me to always make sure Buddy was okay even after Grandpa was gone. So when he died, and I realized that Buddy may have been responsible—purely by accident—I couldn't risk him going to jail."

"So you decided to allow the blame to fall on you. That's crazy."

She stiffened and pushed him, but his arms tightened and he didn't let her go.

"I didn't say *you* were crazy, just that the decision you made was crazy. I can't imagine your grandfather wanting you to sacrifice your future just to keep his best friend from going to jail."

"That's because you didn't know my father," a voice said from the yard. "He was cold and mean, even to those he supposedly loved."

Dex and Amber turned to see Freddie Callahan standing at the bottom of the stairs, in pretty much the same place that Buddy had been standing earlier in the day.

"What is it with you people sneaking up on us all the time?" Dex grumbled.

"What do you want?" Amber said, not sounding particularly welcoming, and Dex couldn't blame her for that. Freddie had never been supportive of Amber and had just insulted the man that Amber held up as her hero.

Freddie held out her hands in a plaintive gesture. "I came to apologize. Amber, I know I always assumed you had something to do with my father's death. But you can't exactly blame me since you ran the way you did. Now that Buddy has explained to everyone what really happened, I'm here to, well, like I said—apologize. I'm sorry that I couldn't support you more. Without knowing the truth, I couldn't. Even though I didn't even like him, he was still my father. And I owed him more loyalty than to welcome back the niece who'd played a role in his death." She held her hands out as if to hug Amber. "But I'd like to welcome you back now. If you'll let me."

Amber leaned into Dex's side. "I don't know that I'm ready for hugs, but if you want to visit, to get to know me better, I'd welcome you into the house." She looked up at the ominous sky. "You might want to hurry before the storm opens up, too."

Freddie looked up at the sky. "You've got that right. This is going to be one for the record books. I can feel it in my bones." She hurried up the steps and Amber led her into the kitchen, with Dex following close behind.

No sooner had they gotten inside than the rain began pouring down so heavily the trees in the backyard were nearly hidden from view.

"Wow," Freddie said. "Good thing I rolled up my windows before parking out front. I rang that doorbell a bunch of times, but you must not have heard it since you were out back."

As if on cue, the doorbell rang. They all hurried through the maze of rooms toward the front of the house. When she opened the door, she was surprised to see Buddy Johnson standing on the porch, along with a young woman of eighteen or nineteen that she didn't recognize.

"Buddy? What can I do for you?"

He motioned to the young brunette beside him. "This is Amy. She works part-time at The Moon and Star and has been covering while Faye and Jake are on their honeymoon. We thought it might be nice to bring you dinner to welcome you back. I hope you don't mind. We thought it would be fun to surprise you."

She stood in the opening, not sure what to do. Yes, she'd taken the blame for her grandfather's death to protect Buddy. But it still stung that no one had questioned her guilt. No one but a stranger named Dex Lassiter.

He chose that moment to put his arm around her shoulder and pull her against his side. "Amber," he whispered, low, "unless you have an ark to put them in to send them back to town I think you might need to step back and let them in."

She sighed and moved aside.

Dex leaned down toward her. "Very nice of you to welcome them," he whispered. "And from the looks of the storm, they might end up being overnight guests."

"Wonderful," she grumbled.

They were about to step back and close the door when a set of headlights appeared from the dark monsoon and inched its way past the other cars to the far end of the porch, where another set of steps angled down from another opening in the railing.

"I don't think I know anyone who arrives in limousines," Amber said. "Must be someone you know."

"Probably Garreth, our attorney."

She smiled at the way he'd said "our" and headed with him down the long porch to where the car had parked. The lights turned off as the driver cut the engine. Then he hopped out in the rain, opened an enormous black umbrella and hurried to the far side to open the door. Three men and a woman scrambled out of the car and hurried up the porch, followed by the driver carrying small bags as if the people planned on staying for a while.

Dex cursed and stopped when he and Amber were still halfway to where the others were. She glanced at him curiously and stopped as well to wait for their newest arrivals to reach them.

"Who are they?" she asked, raising her voice so he could hear her over the rain.

He grabbed her shoulders and turned her to face him. "No matter what, remember what happened between us last night. And what I told you. I care about you, Amber. And I would never cheat on you or anyone else."

She frowned in confusion. What had happened was that they'd made love most of the night. Her face flushed hot at the memory. What did that have to do with these new arrivals? Or anything that he may have told her in the dark? Or...cheating?

He dropped his hands and faced the group as they stopped in front of them.

"Garreth." He shook hands with his attorney. He shook the driver's hand before pulling Amber against his side in a show of affection that had her staring intently at the remaining two men and woman standing there and wondering just what kind of bombshell was about to be dropped on her.

"Mitchell Fielding, Derek Slater." Dex presented the men to Amber. "This is Amber Callahan, owner of this house. And I'm sure that Garreth must have told you she's the one who saved me after the crash."

Amber looked up at Dex expectantly.

"Mitchell is my assistant at Lassiter Enterprises. And Derek is a board member."

"And his wingman." Derek winked at Amber.

"Ah, I see." She really didn't and didn't appreciate the wink, either. But she shook their hands anyway.

"Aren't you going to introduce me, Dex?" The woman beside Mitchell flipped her long, blond hair over her shoulder to hang in a perfect straight sheet cut to razor-sharp precision in the middle of her back. The black dress she wore revealed far more cleavage and leg than Amber had ever dared to bare and had Amber feeling like a worn-out old shoe in comparison. This woman was the epitome of class and chic style, like one of those fancy models on a magazine. She latched on to Dex's arm as if she owned it and rubbed up against him like a well-fed cat, her too-blue-to-be-real eyes narrowing at Amber.

Since Dex seemed to be searching for words, Amber held out her hand. "Hello, I'm Amber Callahan. And you are?"

The woman shook Amber's hand in a noodle-like grip before snatching her hand back and rubbing it on Dex's shirt. "Didn't Dex tell you, darling? I'm Mallory Rothschild. His fiancée."

DEX SIPPED HIS whiskey and Coke and glared out of bleary eyes at Amber on the other side of the massive room that she'd called the great room. The only thing great thing about it was that it was huge and could accommodate the

crazy mixture of Mystic Glades residents plus
his own associates—nine people in all, including him and Amber. She, Freddie and Amy had
spent the past hour getting everyone drinks
and snacks. Dex had never seen anyone more
intent on being a gracious hostess than Amber
was at this minute. And since he already knew
she wasn't keen on any of these people being
here, he knew she was doing it for one reason
and one reason only—to avoid talking to him.

Which was why he was on his third whiskey.

"More, darling?" Mallory purred in her
chair beside him. She held up the decanter.

He slapped his hand over his glass, more to
be obstinate than anything else. "Don't you
have somewhere else you need to go? Like
back to Naples to catch a plane?"

She set the decanter down on the silver tray
and ran her finger across its discolored surface, her perfect nose wrinkling in distaste.
"You know we're all stuck here because of this
storm. You might as well stop being so stub-
born and just accept that we're here for the
duration. Everyone over there—" she waved
airily toward the other side of the room where
Buddy, Freddie and the other Mystic Glades
people were sitting "—said there's no way to
make it back into town in a storm this bad. The
road is bound to be washed out."

"I'm sure Amber probably has a canoe around here somewhere. You're welcome to use it."

She patted his arm. "Stop trying to be funny. It's not working."

He grabbed his glass and downed the last of his drink. "Garreth, I can understand you bringing Mitchell and Derek to go over business matters if there are decisions I need to make. But why exactly did you feel it was a good idea to bring my ex-fiancée?"

Garreth cleared his throat. "Perhaps you can ask Mitchell about that. He's the one who brought her with him to the airport in Saint Augustine."

"Okay. Mitchell. Spill."

"Oh, for goodness' sakes," Mallory said. "Stop talking about me as if I'm not here. Mitchell hasn't severed ties with me like some people around here. And when he heard about the crash he told me about it. Naturally I was worried and wanted to see for myself that you were okay. Is that really so hard to understand? After all, we meant something to each other once. Didn't we?"

The naked pain in her voice had guilt squeezing Dex's chest and made him feel like a heel. He'd never loved her, and she'd never loved him. That wasn't a secret. They'd just latched on to each other for convenience, because talking was easy and they were both getting older. It wasn't until it was time to set the date and make real wedding plans that he'd realized he just couldn't do it and had broken it off. She'd agreed easily enough, almost seeming relieved. Or so he'd thought. Had he been wrong? It had never occurred to him that she might really care about him beyond being a really good friend. But it should have.

"I'm sorry, Mal. For everything."

Her eyes widened as if in surprise before she nodded and turned away. But not before Dex saw the moisture in her eyes. Wonderful. Now he felt like an even greater jerk than he had a moment earlier. When had everything become so screwed up?

His gaze caught Garreth's, who winced and took a sip of his drink—water. Come to think of it, Dex didn't think he'd ever seen his lawyer drink alcohol, but he'd never really thought about it until now.

"Speaking of being concerned about you," Mitchell said as he leaned forward to be seen from Garreth's left. "Veronica Walker stopped at the office asking about you as we were packing our briefcases for the trip out here. She'd heard about the crash on the news and demanded to know if you were okay."

Dex blinked in surprise. "Ronnie asked about me? I find that hard to believe, unless she wanted to come out here with you to make sure I never came back."

Mallory was suddenly just as interested in Mitchell's response as Dex was.

Mitchell cleared his throat, perhaps realizing that this might have been something better left said in private. "Actually, she seemed genuinely concerned. I told her you'd managed to land the plane, more or less, near Mystic Glades and that we were going to check on you." He cleared his throat again. "I didn't tell her anything else."

Dex glanced around the room, toward the windows, suddenly feeling as if a ghost had just danced on his grave. Of all the people he'd want knowing where he was at this very moment, Ronnie was last on his list. The few months they'd dated had started out perfectly, but she'd quickly become possessive and almost...stalkerish. He'd considered getting a restraining order by the time he'd managed to disentangle himself from her clutches. But she'd been more of a nuisance than someone he considered to be dangerous so he hadn't pursued any legal action. He'd just had his security guards at the office keep an eye out for her to insure she didn't get into the building.

And he'd changed his phone numbers. Now, knowing she was still asking about him had him wondering if she knew anything about planes and how to sabotage them.

"Garreth, when we get out of here and have a chance to talk to the NTSB again—"

"I know. Tell them to add Veronica Walker to the list of potential suspects. Will do."

Dex took another gulp of whiskey, feeling increasingly uneasy as he thought about Ronnie. He tried to pretend that Mallory wasn't staring at him curiously and, above all, tried to ignore the urge to run across the room and drag Amber somewhere private so he could try to explain everything to her. But he didn't want to embarrass her, or himself if she refused to talk to him. His shoulders slumped. This whole evening had been a disaster.

He set his drink on a nearby table. "Mitchell, Derek, if you're so inclined, perhaps we can have an impromptu business meeting and I'll look through the papers you brought down for me to sign. May as well do something today to make it not a total waste."

"I'll accompany you, if you don't mind. Just in case I need to review some of those papers," Garreth said.

"Of course." Dex turned to Mallory and put his hand on hers, still feeling guilty. "Good night, Mal. And I really am sorry. I shouldn't have doubted your sincerity in coming out here. Thank you for wanting to check on me."

The look of surprise on her face had him feeling even lower. Just how much of a jerk had he been to her in the past? He'd always thought the breakup was mutual. Now he wondered if he'd mowed over her without even realizing she might have felt differently.

"Good night, Dex," she whispered, looking thoughtful. "See you in the morning."

He nodded, looked toward the other side of the room for Amber and saw her laughing and talking to the young woman who helped out at the Moon and Star, Amy. He shot out of his chair. "Follow me, guys." He stalked through the room, aiming a glare in Amber's direction before heading through the side door into one of the many hallways in the back of the mansion on the west wing.

"Where are we going?" Garreth asked.

"I have no idea. But this mausoleum is big enough that I'm sure we'll find somewhere to sit down with relative privacy if we just get moving." He turned to his right, then to his left when a wall blocked him. A few minutes later he found what was probably a library, based on the number of books on the walls. But it had the main requirement he'd been hoping to find. A fully stocked bar. "Bless you, Grand-daddy Callahan." He strode across the room and grabbed the first bottle he could find.

AMBER QUICKLY ENDED her conversation with Amy, giving her a lame excuse that she needed to use the bathroom. She smiled and nodded at the others as she made her way to the end of the room where her aunt Freddie was standing.

"Do you mind playing hostess for me? I'm afraid I've a bit of a headache. I think I'm going to call it a night."

Freddie patted her shoulder. "Of course. Don't you worry about a thing. I'll just tell everyone to pick a room and make up their own beds. There are dozens of them in this monstrosity. It's all under control. See you in the morning, dear."

She kissed her aunt's cheek, feeling genuine warmth toward her at that moment. She cast a glance toward Dex's fiancée, who was silently sipping her drink and looking lost in thought. Then Amber slipped through the same door-way Dex had a few moments ago.

She didn't know where he'd gone with his lawyer, assistant and board member, and she told herself she didn't care. Which, of course, was a lie. She headed up the main stairs to her room to escape.

THUNDER BOOMED OVERHEAD, startling Dex from his stupor. He jerked upright in his chair and looked around. Still in the library, but he was alone now. He rubbed his eyes and glanced at his watch. Midnight. The business meeting had ended hours ago. Everyone must have either gone back to the great room or found a bedroom to hunker down overnight. It was time that he did the same.

He started down the main hallway back toward the great room but quickly got lost. It took a good half an hour before he found a staircase and started up it. Hopefully, it would lead him back to his own room. If not he'd just commandeer one of the many rooms in the mansion. He tightened his grip around the bottle of whiskey in his hand as he topped the stairs and started in what he believed to be the right direction.

For once, he was right and ended up at his bedroom door. Finally. He shoved the door open and kicked it closed behind him, stumbling to the bathroom. He set the bottle on the sink and took care of nature's call. By then the bottle no longer seemed quite so appealing. He was beginning to feel as green as he probably looked. Just how many glasses had he had tonight? One too many, that was for sure. And he didn't have to guess why he was in such a foul mood. Mallory showing up tonight had made him face things he hadn't wanted to face. It wasn't a good feeling to realize he'd hurt her and, therefore, possibly others. And now he'd hurt the one person he really truly cared about, Amber.

If only he could have gotten Amber alone so he could explain. But as soon as Mallory had introduced herself, Amber had made herself scarce, using the excuse of seeing to her guests.

He looked around the bedroom, which seemed much lonelier now than it had before. Of course, having shared it with Amber, there was no longer any appeal in being alone. He stared at the bedroom door. Amber was just across the hall. If she'd gone to bed by now. Maybe he could talk to her.

He headed across the room, pulled the door open and was inside Amber's room in no time.

She jerked upright in bed, her eyes widening in the glow from the open closet door. Apparently she liked to sleep with a light on. He vaguely wondered how she'd managed to survive in the wilderness all this time if she was afraid of the dark.

"Get out," she ordered.

"Shh." He put his fingers to his lips, or tried

to, but he missed and poked his eye. "Ouch." He cursed and slid to the floor, holding his eye.

"Oh good grief." Amber flipped the covers back and hurried over to him, getting down on her knees beside him. "Let me see." She pulled his hand back, then waved her hand in front of her face and wrinkled her nose. "What did you do, drink an entire bottle of tequila all by yourself?"

He lifted his bottle and shook it. "Whiskey. Good stuff, too. Your grandpa had good taste." He tried to unscrew the cap but couldn't quite manage it. "Will you open it? The damn thing keeps slipping."

She took the bottle from him. "I'll take care of it." She stood and set the bottle on top of a chest of drawers, then reached down for his hand. "Come on. I'll help you find your way back to your room."

He grabbed her hand but, instead of getting up, he yanked her down onto his lap and wrapped his arms around her. "We need to talk."

She shoved against his shoulders and tried to wiggle out of his hold. "I don't talk to drunks, especially when every other word is slurred. I mean it, Dex. Let me go."

Her tone made its way through his stupor

and he dropped his arms. "I'm sorry." He scrubbed his face as she hopped up.

"So am I. Now go. It's late."

He tried to push himself up, but his wobbly legs didn't want to work. He collapsed back against the wall. "Can't I just stay here? I won't be much trouble. Promise."

She rolled her eyes and put her hands on her hips. "Won't Mallory miss you?"

He winced. "That's what I wanted to talk about."

"Well, I don't. If you want to stay, stay. But be quiet. I'm tired and I'm going to sleep." She moved back to the bed and flounced down on the mattress, jerking the covers up around her neck and turning to face the window.

Dex let out a deep sigh and pushed himself on all fours over to her bed. "Amber," he whispered.

"Go away."

"I'm tired. Can I please get in bed with you? The floor is hard."

"Then go to your room and get in that bed."

"It's too far. I don't think I can make it. Please?" Thunder boomed overhead and lightning lit the windows. The rain was coming down even harder than before. "Please? Don't make me sleep alone in the rain."

She flipped her covers back and turned

to glare at him. "You're drunk, Dex. And a cheater. Neither of those make you particularly appealing or make me want to share a bed with you again. Especially not at—" she glanced at the beside clock "—almost one in the morning. Good grief."

He sighed heavily and propped his head on his hands as he rested his elbows on the mattress. "I may be drunk, but I'm not a cheater. Mallory and I used to be engaged. But we broke up. Two months ago."

She narrowed her eyes. "If that's true, why did she introduce herself as your fiancée?"

"Because she hasn't accepted it yet. I'm hard to forget."

She rolled her eyes again and flounced over on her side, facing away from him. "I've already forgotten you, so that can't be true."

"Okay, okay. I think she's mad at me."

"Now, that I believe." Her voice was muffled against her pillow.

"Amber?"

"What?"

"It's a big bed."

"Oh, for the love of… Okay, get into bed. Just stay on your side and leave me alone."

He grinned and slid into bed beside her, right where he wanted to be. He scooted as close to her as he dared, not wanting to make her mad. Then he plopped a kiss on her shoulder. "Good night, sweet Amber."

She wiped her shoulder as if to erase the kiss. "Good night, drunken Dex."

AMBER SIGHED AS Dex's heavy, even breathing told her he'd already passed out. She really should have made him leave. But it was hard to argue with him when he was so adorably drunk and kept giving her puppy-dog eyes.

She was fairly certain he was telling the truth about Mallory being his ex. If he was anything like her, then he wasn't good at lying while intoxicated. Liquor was more likely to loosen lips and make the truth come out than to make someone better at concealing something. And she was more relieved than she probably should have been to learn that Mallory had lied and that they weren't engaged.

She brushed his hair back from his forehead, then smiled when he swatted his face as if to swat a fly. And when he reached for her in his sleep, this time she didn't pull away. She snuggled back against him and pulled his arms around her waist.

Chapter Eleven

Bang!

Amber awoke with a start at the loud noise and was suddenly struggling to breathe as Dex threw himself on top of her, his gaze darting around the room.

"What's going on?" she whispered, as she tried to extricate herself from beneath him, very aware that her nightshirt had ridden up to her belly and that Dex had apparently shed all his clothes except for his boxers during the night.

He glanced down at her as if only just now seeing her, then rolled off her. "Are you okay?"

"I think so. What was that noise?"

"Gunshot."

She stared at him in shock. "Are you sure it wasn't thunder?" As if in response to her question, thunder boomed overhead and another incredible wave of rain began pouring in earnest.

"That sound came from inside the house. Definitely not thunder. And your gun is in my room."

She scooted to the edge of the bed and pulled the drawer open in the side table. "Here." She handed him a Colt .45 revolver.

He shook his head. "Really? How many guns do you have around here?"

She shrugged. "Way of life. The Glades can be a dangerous place. And don't worry about it being rusty with age or anything. I cleaned it earlier, before I went to bed."

"Good to know." He threw his pants on, checked the gun's loading, then hurried to the door and peered out. "Wait here." He locked the door, then shut it behind him.

Amber shook her head. When would the man stop telling her what to do and thinking that he needed to protect her?

She grabbed her pile of clothes from the chair beside the bed and quickly dressed. She was just tugging on her sneakers when a knock sounded on the door.

"It was thunder after all, wasn't it?" She unlocked the door and pulled it open.

Her aunt Freddie stood in the hallway, her face lined with worry. "No, it wasn't thunder."

Amber stepped into the hall, surprised to see a small group of people milling around the doorway across from her. The door to Dex's room.

"What's going on?" she asked. She didn't wait for her aunt's reply because she saw Dex coming out of the room with Buddy and two of the men who had arrived in the limo yesterday—Derek and Mitchell.

She hurried to Dex, but he quickly closed the door, blocking her view. He tested the knob, perhaps making sure he'd locked it as he'd closed it.

"Stay back," he said. "Everyone get back. We need to preserve the scene for the police." He motioned the increasingly growing group of people back, as others followed the noise to the upstairs corridor.

"What scene? What happened?" Amber asked.

"It's Mallory," he said, his voice tight. "Someone killed her."

She gasped and motioned toward the door. "In your room?"

He nodded.

Buddy put his hand on Dex's shoulder. "I don't think it was Mr. Lassiter, though. He was just reaching the door when I topped the stairs."

"Maybe he'd just come out of the room," Freddie said. "After all, it was his bedroom."

Mitchell and Derek shared a surprised glance, as if only just now considering that Dex might have been involved.

Amber held up her hands. "You can stop that rumor right now. Dex was with me, in my room, when a gunshot rang out. He's not the one who killed Mallory." She looked to Dex. "I'm assuming she was shot?"

"Yes." His voice was tight, clipped, making Amber wonder if he still harbored some feelings for his ex-fiancée after all. Then again, if they'd been engaged to be married, of course he would still have some kind feelings for her.

She grabbed his hand and held it tightly in hers. When he looked down at her, she silently mouthed the words, *I'm sorry.*

He squeezed her hand in response, then let it go. "Does anyone have a cell phone?"

Buddy handed him his. "Not that you'll get a call out in this storm. Even the areas that get coverage around here, like this house, usually don't work in storms. Don't know why. But you can try."

Sure enough, the call wouldn't go through. He handed the phone back to Buddy. "If anyone else has a phone, maybe with a different carrier, can you please try calling nine-one-one?"

Aunt Freddie tried, and so did Mitchell and

Derek. Both of them shook their heads after trying to get a call out.

"Okay," Dex said. "We all need to assemble in one place so we can verify that everyone is safe and accounted for. Who all are missing?"

Aunt Freddie held up her hands and started counting off her fingers. "There should be eight of us now, minus Miss Rothschild. But I only count seven. Someone's missing. And it's not one of us locals." The tone of her voice said what she hadn't, that it made sense to her that the missing person—allegedly the killer— would *not* be one of the Mystic Glades residents.

Dex looked around. "It's Garreth. Does anyone know what bedroom he was staying in?"

Derek shoved to the front of the group. "He was in the room next to mine, in the east wing. Come on. I'll show you."

He led them down the hall, past the staircase. Bare feet and shoes clomped and shuffled against the hardwood floor as the entire herd followed them. When they arrived at the closed door, Dex motioned for everyone to stay back as he drew the Colt from his waistband and reached for the knob.

A flurry of activity and noise had him looking back over his shoulder. His mouth dropped open when he realized that the locals, except for Amber, were now holding guns and pointing them at the same door he was about to open. Even Amy, who didn't look old enough to be out of high school, was pointing a pistol at the door.

"Good grief," he said. "Where did you all get those?"

Buddy gave him a confused look. "We always carry guns when we go deep into the Glades, and this house is as deep as we go."

"Well, point them somewhere else. I don't want to get shot."

Buddy looked sheepish and lowered his gun, then motioned for the others to do the same. Mitchell and Derek stood away from the others, looking as shocked as Dex felt. And none of them had guns. The theory that the killer wasn't a local looked pretty flimsy to Dex, considering only the Mystic Glades people were armed. And how would someone in his group have brought a gun out here after flying down from Saint Augustine? They couldn't have gotten any guns through security.

Even Garreth, who'd been here a day longer than the others, couldn't have brought a gun. And Dex couldn't imagine him running out and buying one in Naples. There was no way his staid, serious lawyer who saw only right and wrong with no gray areas would ever consider buying a gun. And he certainly had no reason to kill Mallory.

Dex knocked on the door and shoved his own borrowed gun back into his waistband, feeling silly for even having it out in the first place. Garreth wasn't a killer. Period.

"Garreth? It's Dex. Are you in there?" He knocked again. "Garreth?"

"He's probably done run off," Freddie said. "After shooting that lady friend of yours."

"He's a lawyer who has dedicated his life to the pursuit of the law. He's not a murderer," Dex said.

"So you say." As one, all the locals nodded as if to lend their belief to hers. Including Amber this time.

Dex rolled his eyes and knocked on the door again. "Garreth?" When his lawyer didn't answer, Dex turned the knob, then pushed the door open. He stepped inside as Garreth bolted up in the bed, staring at him in alarm.

"What's going on?" He pulled a pair of earplugs out of his ears and looked in shock first at the gun in Dex's waistband and then past him.

Dex didn't have to turn around to know that his band of followers in the hallway were probably all crowded around the doorway peeking inside, if they hadn't already come inside.

"There's been a shooting," he said. "You didn't hear anything?"

Garreth held out the earplugs. "No. Was someone hurt?"

"Mallory. She's…dead."

Garreth's mouth fell open and his face turned pale. "Mallory's dead?" he choked. He cleared his throat. "I don't understand. What happened?" He tossed his earplugs onto the bedside table and grabbed his robe from the foot of the bed, tugging it on and tying the belt.

"Good question. Looks like now that we've found you, everyone is accounted for. Which means either there was an intruder, or—"

"Or one of us is the killer," Garreth said.

Dex nodded. "We need to corral everyone somewhere, take away their guns—"

"Guns?"

"It seems to be standard issue out here. They all have them."

Garreth's gaze dropped to Dex's waistband, his eyes widening. "Including you."

"I borrowed it. After I heard the gunshot."

The color began returning to Garreth's face and he straightened his shoulders, looking all business again. "As your lawyer, I strongly recommend that you return the gun to whomever you borrowed it from. It could likely be the murder weapon and since you'd be the first suspect, given that the victim is—"

"He didn't kill her." Amber stood beside Dex. "And that gun was in my drawer in my room when the gunshot went off. It can't be the murder weapon."

Garreth looked pointedly at how close Amber was standing next to Dex and frowned. "Given that Miss Callahan was only recently suspected of murder herself, I suggest that you keep your distance from her. It doesn't look right."

Dex put his arm around Amber's shoulders. "That little bit of advice isn't going to be followed. My suggestion is that you get dressed. We'll all meet in, um, the…" He glanced down at Amber and arched a brow.

"In the great room where we were last night. It's at the front of the house, to the left of the front door. It's close to the kitchen so we can fix coffee or sodas for everyone."

"Right. The great room. We'll see you there."

Garreth grabbed his cell phone from beside his bed.

"Don't bother," a chorus of people called out from the doorway. "No service."

Dex held Amber's hand and made his way through the throng and headed toward the stairs. "We're going to the great room and we'll figure out what to do," he announced to the others.

"Follow Dex and Amber," Buddy announced. "Dex is Jake's friend, and a private investigator. He'll know what to do and he'll be able to figure out who the bad guy is."

"He's also a sheriff's deputy. He was deputized in town before he came out here," Amber added, as if to give him some legitimacy.

Dex rolled his eyes again but since everyone was following him without complaint, maybe using his temporary deputy status was a good idea. He flipped on lights as the group tromped and clomped through the hallway then down the stairs into the massive two-story foyer.

When they reached the great room, Dex spotted a trunk with a lock on it. "Amber, do you have the key to that trunk?"

She shook her head. "I don't think so."

Buddy hurried to the medieval-sized fireplace at the end of the room and pulled a picture on hinges away from the wall. On the back was a hook with a small ring of keys. "It should be one of these."

"Well, that's a dandy place to hide keys," Dex grumbled. "A burglar would find that in no time."

Buddy handed him the keys and gave him an admonishing look. "We don't have burglars in Mystic Glades. And until tonight, we didn't have murderers, either."

"Too bad you didn't make that clear back when Granddaddy Callahan died and everyone blamed Amber." Dex leaned forward and snatched the keys from Buddy's hand.

Buddy turned red.

Amber stepped between them. "Stop it. There's no point in rehashing the past. And it was just as much my decision to leave after Grandpa died as it was Buddy's to not speak about what he thought happened. We both made mistakes."

Dex didn't understand how she could be so forgiving of her fellow townspeople after being ostracized for two years, but he respected her wishes to drop it and didn't say anything else. He bent down in front of the trunk and tried several keys before one fit. When he opened the trunk, he found it half-full of blankets, with plenty of room for his purposes. He stood and held his hand out to Buddy, who was still looking sullen and standing a few feet away.

"I think we'll all be safer if we lock up the guns. Buddy, you first." He held out his hand.

Buddy looked at him as if he thought he'd lost his mind. "I don't think so."

Amber put her hand on Buddy's shoulder. "Dex is right. Like it or not, someone in this room shot Mallory. We need to lock all the guns away both as evidence and to insure that no one else gets hurt."

"If someone wants to kill one of us, they can do it with or without a gun," he grumbled.

"Buddy," Amber admonished.

"Okay, okay." He pulled his gun out of his waistband and handed it to Dex.

"Thank you." Dex used one of the smaller blankets as a glove of sorts so he didn't touch the gun. He put the gun in the trunk.

Freddie and Amy put their guns in the trunk, as well. And, finally, Dex put his borrowed Colt .45 in with the others. As he locked the trunk, a feeling of relief settled over him. Knowing no one was running around with a loaded gun made him feel much less worried.

"Are there any more guns in the house, Amber?" He didn't bother mentioning the one that may or may not be in her grandfather's sealed room and knew she wouldn't either.

"I don't think so, at least not that I know of."

Buddy walked to the fireplace at the end of the room. "I'll start a fire. It'll be cozy and good to have in case the lights go out. Although the generators should kick in. But you never know."

"I'll help," Aunt Freddie said.

They both began loading kindling and logs

from a wooden box to the right of the hearth. Everyone else split off into groups, sitting on the various chairs and couches around the room.

Dex led Amber to one of the front windows. "If one of us drives into town, do you think we could get phone service there to call the police?"

She shook her head. "Even if we could get service somewhere in town, it wouldn't matter. No one can leave here until this weather clears up."

He gave her an exasperated look. "I'm not afraid of a little rain and lightning."

"You don't understand. Rain like this, for as long as it's been raining, will make the roads impassable. This house and the surrounding property become an island. There's no way to get into town."

"How can you be sure?"

She let out a deep sigh. "Come on. I'll show you." She headed toward the foyer.

"Should we come, too?" Buddy called out.

"No, no. We'll be right back," Dex assured him.

When they reached the front door, Amber opened a drawer in a small decorative table against the wall and pulled out a flashlight.

"Let's hope the batteries still work or that

Buddy has kept fresh ones stocked as part of watching after the estate." She pressed the button. The flashlight remained dark. "One more chance." She reached into the back of the drawer and pulled out a pack of batteries. "Voilà." She exchanged the old batteries for new and the flashlight sparked to life.

"Come on, outsider. I'll prove my point."

He shook his head and followed her to the railing.

She aimed the flashlight toward the front yard and slowly moved it from the trees to the left, across the road, to the trees to the right. Except there wasn't a road anymore. There was a river, flowing left to right and forming a moat around the property.

Dex clutched the railing. "That's crazy. We're stranded."

"Totally. Don't worry, the water won't get into the house. The foundation is on concrete pylons driven deep into the ground. The water would have to rise another six feet to come inside. And as far as I know, it's never gotten that high. Grandpa knew what he was doing when he built this place."

"How long before the water recedes?"

"A good twenty-four hours after the rain stops. Like it or not, we're all stuck here together. With a dead body."

"And a murderer."

She set the flashlight on the railing and faced him. "While we've got a moment alone, tell me what you saw in your bedroom."

"Why?"

"Because I want to know the details and you wouldn't let me in the room. It's my house now. I have a right to know what happened."

"I suppose you do. Okay. Mallory was lying in my bed, under the covers, facing the other way. I didn't know who was in the bed at first. Her hair was covered by a blanket. All I saw was blood." He swallowed hard. "Buddy and I both ran in together and I soon realized it was Mallory. There was no point in performing CPR. She was already dead, and the bullet did…too much damage."

She seemed to think about what he'd said for a moment. "I think you need to consider that whoever killed your fiancée—"

"Ex-fiancée."

"—might have been trying to kill you, instead."

"Because she was in my bedroom?"

"Yes. Everyone knew where you and I were staying because we'd already claimed those rooms and told the others to choose different ones. And someone did sabotage your plane. If

Mallory was under the covers, the killer might have thought it was you."

"Makes sense. Makes more sense than someone wanting to kill Mallory. No one here has any reason to want her harmed."

"Are you sure about that? Did they all know her very well?"

He frowned. "Derek knew her, of course, since we double-dated in the beginning. But I don't think he kept in touch with her after we broke up. Mallory did mention last night that she'd heard about the plane crash from Mitchell. That surprised me, since I wouldn't have expected that Mitchell and she would have had anything to do with each other after we ended the engagement."

"And Garreth?"

"He was going to be the best man at the wedding, so of course he knew Mallory. But he didn't have any reason to want her dead."

"What about you?"

"What about me?"

"Your lawyer seemed concerned that someone might think you had something to do with her murder."

"He's just being protective since I'm his client. But I had no reason to want her dead."

"Are you sure?"

He tightened his hands on the railing. "What

exactly about me makes you think I'd kill someone? Especially a woman I was going to marry?"

She met his stare without flinching. "Since you were in my room when she was killed, I obviously know that you didn't harm her. What I'm asking is whether anyone else would have reason to suspect you'd want to kill her."

His anger faded as he considered what she was saying. "You think someone killed her to frame me?"

She shrugged. "Just looking at all of the possibilities."

"Maybe I should change Lassiter and Young Private Investigations to Lassiter and Callahan."

She grinned. "Maybe you should."

Lightning cracked across the sky, briefly illuminating the growing river like a strobe light. "Standing out here doesn't feel too safe right now. I think we might be better off taking our chances inside. Come on."

They'd just stepped inside when the lights went out.

Chapter Twelve

Dex stood on the back porch beside Garreth, Amber and Buddy, eyeing the swirling, brackish water that covered the fifty yards between the house and the maintenance shed. Conveniently, the shed—which housed the generator—was on pylons, which meant it was above the water level, but inconveniently, it was still through the swamp.

"I don't suppose the rain and lightning will keep the snakes away." Dex stared at the dark water.

"Or the alligators," Garreth added.

"Probably not," Amber agreed. "Honestly, there's no reason to go out there. We've got plenty of firewood and candles for light. And it's not exactly cold outside. We'll all just sweat a bit with the air conditioner off."

Dex grimaced. "Speaking of sweating, and no airconditioning, if we're going to be stuck in this house much longer, there's something else to worry about." He grimaced and looked at Amber. "Mallory. We need to do something to…" He swallowed hard. "Preserve her."

"Oh. I hadn't thought of that. Well, there is a deep freeze in the kitchen. I suppose we could, ah, empty it and…"

"I suppose we could," Dex agreed, bile rising up in his throat at the idea of putting his former fiancée's body in a freezer. Even though they hadn't loved each other, they had been friends. And the idea that someone had killed her had him clenching his fists and wishing for someone to punch. "All right. That alone means I have to get that generator going. Buddy, you said any tools I might need are in the shed, too. What about fuel for the generator?"

"The fuel is in a tank on the far side, outside the structure. I'm sure it's full. The problem is more likely a fuse. All this lightning must have overloaded a circuit."

Dex stripped out of his jeans down to his boxers, then pulled on his tennis shoes, which he'd grabbed from upstairs. He took the keys out of his pocket. "Amber, we'll need that flashlight. Maybe Buddy can shine it on the water so I can see where I'm going. And will you unlock the trunk and grab the .45? You'll be on snake-and-gator patrol while I swim over."

"This is crazy, Dex. It's too dangerous. You

have no way of knowing what's in that water. And as fast as it's moving it could suck you out into the swamp."

"I don't have a choice. I can't let…Mallory… I have to get the generator on. Okay?"

She sighed. "Okay. I get it. Just give me a minute."

She ran inside and returned shortly with the gun. She checked the loading, then held it down by her side. "Ready."

Dex leaned down to press a quick kiss against her lips, but she put her hand around his neck and pulled him in for a deeper kiss full of longing. When she broke the kiss, his traitorous body was straining against the front of his boxers. He shook his head and grinned.

"You're dangerous, Amber."

She stepped closer, shielding him from the others. There was no sign of humor on her face though as she looked up at him. "Be careful, Dex. I mean it. If you get in that water and the current is too strong, get out. No heroics. It's not worth it."

"Are you saying you'd miss me if something happened to me?" he teased.

"Yes."

Her quick, serious answer had his body tightening almost painfully. "There's no way in hell that I won't come back to you." He kissed her again, then headed down the porch steps before she could try to stop him. As soon as Buddy shone the flashlight on the roiling water at the base of the steps, Dex stepped into the abyss.

The water wasn't overly deep, only up to his hips. But Amber was right. The current was incredibly strong as water rushed from the surrounding higher areas and was sucked out toward the Glades. Every step was a struggle to remain upright, and soon he was sweating and breathing heavily as if he'd been in a tremendous battle. But other than dodging some dead branches floating past him, he made it to the maintenance shed without incident.

He pulled himself up on the concrete steps, catching his breath as he looked back toward the house. Amber waved at him and he waved back to let her know all was well. Then he opened the door and went inside. Too late he realized he should have brought a flashlight. The interior was as dark as midnight. He ran his hands along the wall until he located the light switch and flipped it. Nothing.

He felt along the walls for a fuse box, and tripped over several tools and unknown objects before he found it. Not wanting to stick his wet hands inside the box, he felt around for a while until he found a bucket of rags and wiped his hands dry. Then he returned to the box and carefully patted the interior until he found the main switch. He shoved it up until it clicked, then pulled it back down to reset everything. Since he didn't hear the hum of the generator outside kicking on, he started flipping each breaker individually. Halfway through, the generator suddenly belched to life.

Dex shut the panel, went back to where he remembered the light switch being and flipped it on. A single, dim light popped to life overhead, revealing an incredibly unorganized pile of tools, old paint cans, a riding lawn mower and hundreds of other odds and ends. He grabbed a machete out of one pile and hefted it in his hand. If it came to a fight with an alligator or a snake, that machete would be good to have. But it also wasn't something he wanted in the house for the killer to get a hold of. The idea of someone like Amber coming up against a weapon like that had him leaving it where he'd found it. Too dangerous. He couldn't risk it. He'd just have to brave the waters outside again and hope he was as lucky the second time as he had been the first—that he'd encounter no wildlife of the slithering or biting variety.

When he went outside, he noticed Amber

and Buddy still waiting for him, but Garreth was nowhere to be seen. Maybe he'd had to flip fuses inside the house? Lights shone from both the first and second floors, so the generator was definitely doing its job. And he could see the silhouettes of several people in the kitchen behind the porch.

He studied the brackish water for any sinister shadows beneath the surface or the shine of snake scales, then waded back in. If anything, the current was stronger this time. And the water had risen noticeably and was now halfway up his chest. By the time he struggled to the porch steps, he saw the water was cresting just below the second highest step, a foot below where the bottom floor began. Amber's worried gaze confirmed his own fears as he emerged from the water.

"Has it ever gotten this high before?" he asked.

"Not that I know of," Buddy interjected, clicking off the flashlight.

Amber agreed and handed Dex a towel to dry off. "I think we might need to move everyone upstairs, just in case."

"I think you're right." He motioned toward the kitchen door. "What's going on in there?"

Amber gave him a haunted look. "Garreth is directing everyone to empty out the freezer."

He gave her a tight nod and pulled on his jeans before pulling his T-shirt on over his head.

When they went inside, Dex stopped in surprise. Everyone was sitting around the huge kitchen island. Stacks of pints of ice cream formed a mound in the middle and the group was sorting through them, apparently grabbing their favorites.

Mitchell handed a chocolate-mint pint to Amy and she gave him a shy smile in return. Derek shoved a spoonful of Moose Tracks into his mouth, then held out his hands in a helpless gesture.

Garreth looked disgusted with all of them as he leaned against the kitchen wall like a general watching over his unruly troops.

Freddie motioned toward the refrigerator. "We put most of the veggies in the refrigerator freezer, but there wasn't anywhere to store all this ice cream. Might as well enjoy it before it goes to waste, right?"

Dex's stomach clenched with nausea and he headed through the archway without a word.

Amber hurried behind him and caught up to him when he was at the bottom of the stairs.

"What's wrong?" she asked.

He looked down at her. "It just seems… disrespectful, to sit there enjoying ice cream, knowing the reason it was taken out of the freezer." He shrugged and headed up the stairs. "Stupid, I know."

She hurried after him. "Not stupid at all. I totally get it. Where are we going?"

"I'm getting a shower to clean all that swamp muck off me."

"Okay. But what are you going to wear?"

He stopped at the top of the stairs, his gaze shooting to the closed door on his room. "Good point. I need my suitcase." His steps were much slower as he approached the door. "Do you still have that ring of keys?"

She pulled them out of her pocket and held up the skeleton key.

"Thanks. Here, hold this while I go inside." He handed her the gun.

She looked around the dark hallway. "Hurry," she whispered. "It seems creepy up here now, you know."

"Believe me. I know." He unlocked the door and rushed inside, keeping his gaze averted from the bed.

Once he had his suitcase, he was just about to step into the hall when movement off to his left had him whirling around. The room was empty. There was no one there, no one except… Mallory. He glanced quickly to the bed, as if to assure himself she was still there and hadn't become some disembodied ghost haunting the mansion. She still lay in the center of the bed where he'd found her. He swallowed hard and looked away. He stood there for a full minute, trying to figure out what he'd seen.

"Dex?" Amber's voice called to him from the hallway. "Is something wrong?"

Yes. But what? What had he seen out of the corner of his eye?

"Dex?"

"Coming." He left the room and locked the door behind him.

AMBER STOOD IN the opening between the great room and the kitchen, facing the great room and keeping the others from going into the kitchen. Not that anyone else wanted to, but Dex was being his usual protective self and obviously wanted her where he could see her, but didn't want her to be a part of what he and his fellow outsiders were doing—storing Mallory's body in the freezer.

There hadn't been the need for a discussion about who would take care of the task. The Mystic Glades residents had respectfully kept their distance while the outsiders took care of one of their own, gently wrapping Mallory in the comforter from the bed upstairs and then carefully carrying her downstairs in a solemn procession that had reminded Amber of a funeral.

The top of the freezer clicked into place in the kitchen behind her, and soon she heard the sounds of the men taking turns washing their hands at the sink. Then, without a word, Garreth, Mitchell and Derek filed past her into the great room, each of them looking deflated and depressed.

Dex stopped beside her, crossing his arms as he surveyed the room.

"Are you okay?" she whispered.

"I will be. I didn't expect it to hurt so much, putting her in there." His voice was too low for the others to hear, but even so she could hear the pain behind his words.

She sidled closer until her hip pressed against the side of his thigh, offering him comfort with that one small touch. "I'm here for you."

He let out a shuddering breath. "I know. Thank you."

Thunder boomed overhead, making her jump. "Good grief. I can't believe this rain." As if remembering the rising flood in the backyard at the same time, they both turned around and headed to the back porch.

"What's up?" Buddy called out, hurrying to

catch up to them. He stopped on the porch beside the two of them. "Oh, my God."

The water was lapping against the edges of the porch boards.

"We have to go upstairs. Now," Amber declared.

They all hurried back inside, but Dex hesitated and glanced at the freezer.

Amber put her hand on his arm. "There's nothing we can do now. The lower floor is about to flood."

"I can't just let…" He rushed past her to the great room. "All right, everyone. The water is rising and is about to come into the house." A collective gasp went up around the room. "We'll need to head upstairs. But first, everyone grab what you can from the pantry. Grab things we can eat and drink without having to cook. Don't forget cups, plates, utensils. Garbage bags would be good too. Hurry."

There was a big rush into the kitchen and everyone started grabbing things from the pantry.

"Amber, we'll need can openers. And is there something we could use to heat beans or anything in cans?"

"I think there's a hot plate." She grabbed Amy as she headed past her. "Amy, help me find it, okay? I think it's over in one of these cabinets." She and Amy rummaged through the cabinets and found two hot plates and a can opener. Amy ran through the great room to the stairs to take them up.

Amber looked around for Dex and froze when she saw what he was doing. He'd gathered his friends and they were wrestling with the heavy freezer, lifting it on top of the marble-topped island. Their muscles bulged and strained as they moved it into place.

Amber noted they'd had to unplug it. The cord dangled over the side. She grabbed an extension cord out of the pantry, sliding past Buddy as he made a second run for more food. She plugged the cord into an outlet above the sink, wrapped most of the extra slack around the freezer handle to keep it from dragging on the floor, then plugged the freezer's cord into it.

The freezer hummed to life. Dex pulled her against him in a fierce hug, then kissed the top of her head. When he pulled back, he framed her face in his hands. "You're a wonderful person, Amber Callahan. Thank you. Again."

She smiled, then let out a little squeak as water began soaking into her shoes. "The water's coming in. Hurry up, everybody. We have to get upstairs."

Everyone made a last dash to the pantry,

then ran through the great room, through the maze, to the stairs. The water was already coming in through the front door, too, and seeping in through the walls.

Dex ushered everyone from the room, waiting until they were all safely out of the kitchen and on their way toward the stairs before joining Amber at the archway. He put his hand on her back, encouraging her forward, but she froze and looked back at the great room.

Dex turned around, shoving her behind him as he looked for the threat.

"Dex, the trunk, the trunk."

He frowned back at her and she pointed to the trunk over by the fireplace. The one with the guns locked inside. Except it wasn't locked anymore, and the lid was standing open.

She and Dex splashed through the water that was already up to their ankles and reached the trunk at the same time.

The guns were gone.

Chapter Thirteen

Amber perched on the edge of a wing chair by the window in the house's second library, the upstairs one, while Dex finished making his rounds on the other side of the room, insuring everyone was okay. Like the great room, the east wing library had plenty of seating, but it was spread out in small groups throughout the stacks of bookshelves so that not everyone was visible at once. That's why Amber had chosen these specific two wing chairs for her and Dex—because at least there was no one behind them, just a floor-to-ceiling bookshelf. Ten feet away, the bookshelf ended and there was an aisle that opened up, like a hallway in the middle of the room. She kept watching that dark opening while trying to keep an eye on Dex.

He finished speaking to Freddie and Buddy, who were seated to the right of the door that led into the hall, nodded at Mitchell, who was curling up to go to sleep on one of the couches, and headed toward Amber.

He glanced toward the bookshelf behind them, perhaps to make sure no one could possibly squeeze behind it to listen to them, and took his seat. They both leaned toward each other, but they continued to watch the others.

"What did you find out?" she said, keeping her voice low.

"I didn't want to announce the guns were missing, because I didn't want to cause a panic. Instead, I was more subtle, or tried to be, asking each person if they were okay, if they'd gotten what they needed from downstairs." He motioned to the stacks of goods everyone had deposited in the common area against one wall, their new pantry, essentially.

"I'm guessing no one admitted to sneaking into the great room and breaking into the trunk."

"Well, I didn't think they would. But based on what everyone said, I was able to pretty much corroborate most of their stories. I'm ruling out Amy, Freddie and Derek. And, of course, you and me. But so far I can't prove the rest of them didn't have an opportunity to get to that trunk. The lock was busted, which implies the thief didn't have a key. But the only person who did have the key was me, so that doesn't help."

"Aren't you ruling out Buddy?"

He shook his head. "No. I can't. No one seems to remember seeing him carrying anything but a case of water upstairs. If he wasn't carrying other things, then where was he while the others were in the pantry?"

She stared across the room at Buddy and Freddie, who were sitting on opposite ends of a couch now, eyes closed, apparently falling asleep sitting up. "I just can't imagine that Buddy would take the guns. Assuming that the person who took the guns is the killer, why would Buddy shoot Mallory? He didn't know her. And if you're the true target, which seems likely, then again, Buddy barely knows you. What motive would he have to want you dead?"

"Okay, with me as the target, who stands to gain something by my death? It would make sense that only Garreth, Derek and Mitchell should be the true suspects. I pay each of them a healthy salary, with excellent benefits. Even Garreth, who takes other clients besides me, earns a generous retainer whether he does work for me each week or not. And our contract pays him escalating amounts above the retainer if he ends up working full-time on any particular issue. With me out of the picture, he'd be at the mercy of my replacement, who might very well hire a different lawyer for future work. I just don't see him gaining anything with me gone."

"All right. Makes sense. As long as the gain is financial. Have you done something to him that might make him want revenge?"

He laughed. "Revenge? Garreth? We're not exactly drinking buddies. It's all business. If anyone had revenge on their mind it would be Derek. We've both dated the same women before, although not at the same time, of course."

She rolled her eyes. "Of course."

He grinned. "There's been some jealousy in the past, on his part. He claims sometimes women see me and leave him because of my money."

"Is that true?"

He shrugged. "Probably. But we usually end up laughing and drinking over the memories later. So far neither of us has been particularly successful in the relationship department, long-term."

"Was Mallory one of the women you both dated?"

He shook his head. "No. She was my mistake alone." He grimaced. "Sorry, that sounds callous now. There've only been a couple of women we've actually both dated. The last was Ronnie—Veronica Walker. She was a bit…aggressive. It took some convincing before she understood that it was really over. I considered a restraining order until she finally quit coming around. I heard Derek dated her a few times after I broke up with her. But, as far as I know, that was very brief."

Amber tapped the arm of her chair and considered what he'd said. "Okay, so Garreth has no obvious reason to want you dead and seems to benefit more with you healthy. Derek is a friend and you've had some quibbles in the past, but it doesn't seem to have impacted your friendship or his position on your board. You did say he was a board member?"

"Yeah. He's one hell of a smart guy. He sits on several boards, not just mine."

"Does he get to run the company with you out of the picture?"

He smiled. "That's not how it works. For one thing, it's privately owned, not publicly traded. So the company would pass to my benefactor in my will."

"Who's your benefactor?"

"Jake Young."

"Faye's Jake?"

"One and the same. He doesn't know he's

the benefactor, though. I'm sure he assumes I've willed my assets to my family."

"Your family?"

"Mother, father, brother. All of them live in California. I haven't seen them in years. And there's no reason to talk about them."

She disagreed, but since they were trying to solve a murder, she was willing to let it drop for now. "Then we've got one more person to consider—Mitchell."

Dex grew quiet and stared out the window. Was he thinking about his family? Or was he maybe thinking that Mitchell was their best suspect? She gave him a minute, but when he didn't respond, she waved her hand in front of his face.

"Dex? We were talking about Mitchell. Do you think he could be our suspect?"

He turned to look at her, his eyes dark, troubled. "As a matter of fact, I do. Mitchell's been my assistant for a couple of years, but I don't know much about his private life. Except for one thing. He was infatuated with Mallory." He waved his hand as if to dispel any bad thoughts she had. "We didn't both date her or anything like that. I brought her to an outside-the-office company event where everyone brought their families or dates."

"Like a company picnic?"

"More or less, a get-to-know-you kind of thing, supposed to make teams work better together according to a consultant who recommended that I do those. We hold them twice a month, usually at a restaurant. But sometimes we'll go to a movie or bowling or something like that. Just the top execs and their families, about twenty-five or thirty people at any particular outing. I remember Mitchell being like a puppy dog following Mallory around that first time. When she mentioned it to me later, I didn't think much of it. But he did it again, at another event, and I had to tell him to leave her alone."

"How did he take that?"

"As you'd expect. He's a grown man. He was embarrassed and resentful but got over it fairly quickly. Or, at least, I'd thought he had. When he found out that I'd broken up with Mallory, I remember hearing from one of the other guys that Mitchell called her to offer his sympathies and a shoulder if she ever needed it. I remember thinking that was a bit odd, to offer your boss's ex-fiancée a shoulder to cry on. Especially when the two of them weren't even close."

"Sounds kind of creepy."

"Yeah, knowing that Mallory's dead now, murdered, it seems way creepy." He glanced around the room. "And I don't have a clue where Mitchell is right now." He suddenly rose from his chair and held out his hand. "Let's get out of here. We're both tired after not getting much sleep last night. And I'd feel a lot safer closing my eyes with a locked door between us and whoever has those guns—whether it's Mitchell or someone else."

THERE WAS NO passion or heat between them this time. They were both far too tired for that. But nothing felt better to Amber than being curled up in Dex's arms on the big, soft feather bed in her room. It had only taken a few minutes for both of them to fall asleep, and she'd slept better than she had in years, feeling safer than she ever had, even knowing that Mallory's killer was still in the house somewhere. The door was locked, her Colt .45 was sitting on the bedside table. She had no reason to worry, as long as they were cocooned in here together.

Or, at least, she shouldn't. But something had jerked her out of a sound sleep, and she had no clue what it was. The sunlight against the window blinds, what little peeked through the cloudy skies outside that were still dumping rain down on them, told her it was probably already afternoon. But the sun wasn't bright enough to have woken her. So what had?

Dex's arms tightened around her and his mouth moved close to her ear. "You heard it, too?" he whispered. "Close your eyes. Pretend you're asleep."

She squeezed his hand around her waist to let him know that she'd heard him, and she kept her eyes closed, breathing deep and even.

The tiniest creak, like a squeaky door hinge, sounded from across the room.

Suddenly Dex jumped out of the bed. Amber opened her eyes just in time to see him disappearing through an opening in the far wall, his footsteps echoing back to her. She blinked in shock as she realized what she was looking at was a hidden door, much like the small panels her grandpa had for storing things in the walls. But this opening was large enough for people. It looked like a hallway. She turned and reached for the gun on the table, but it was gone. She curled her fingers into her palms. *Please let it be Dex who took the gun.*

She hopped out of bed and ran to the opening. It wasn't completely dark. A wall sconce about ten feet in cast more shadow than light, but it allowed her to see enough to realize what she was looking at. She'd lived in this house off and on for years and had never realized it had secret passageways. Was that how the killer had shot Mallory and disappeared so quickly? Had he discovered one of the openings and used it to get in and out of her room?

"Dex?" she whispered, in case he was still close enough to hear her. No answer. And she couldn't hear footsteps, either.

She couldn't believe he'd chased whoever had opened that panel. It was foolhardy and dangerous. And brave. She couldn't fault him for that. He wanted to catch the killer as much as she did, but he should have waited for her. She knew this house inside and out. Okay, not the secret passageway, or passageways, but she knew the rest of the house. Dex didn't. If he went through another panel he might get lost in a part of the house he'd never been in. And he was following a killer who had at least four guns—the one he'd used to kill Mallory, plus those that Amy, Aunt Freddie and Buddy had given up.

She had to help him.

She ran to her dresser and grabbed some jeans and a T-shirt and quickly tugged them on. Then she took the only weapon that she had, her knife, and attached the sheath at her waist. Bringing a knife to a gunfight wasn't the best possible scenario, but at least it gave her a chance. She drew a deep breath, then stepped into the passageway.

DEX FLATTENED HIMSELF against the wall, the revolver in his hand as he inched toward the next turn. He'd only caught glimpses of the person he was following, but he'd seen enough to know that he was definitely chasing a man—which ruled out Aunt Freddie and Amy, not that he'd really considered them suspects. But he was also chasing a young man, which ruled out Buddy, and he was chasing someone over six feet, close to his own height of six-two, which ruled out Derek, who was an inch shy of the six foot mark. That left only two possibilities—his assistant or his lawyer. Both of those possibilities left a bitter taste in his mouth. He'd trusted them with some of the most intimate and important details of his life, and one of them had betrayed him in the worst way, by killing an innocent woman. And now, whoever was stalking these dark halls had committed another sin—he'd threatened Amber by opening that panel into their room.

Dex hadn't been taking the search for the killer all that seriously, hoping to just wait it out until the storm cleared and the water level went down and they could get the police in here to take over. But now he realized he couldn't risk waiting any longer. He had to step up his game and figure out who was behind everything. Waiting and risking that Amber might get hurt—or worse—was unacceptable.

He tightened his hold on his gun and ducked down to make himself less of a target, then whirled around the corner, pointing the gun out in front of him. There, the silhouette of a man at the far end of the passageway ducked back behind the corner.

"Throw your gun out and give up, Mitchell," Dex called out, making a guess as to the identity.

Laughter echoed back to him, then the sound of running feet.

Damn. What did that mean? That it wasn't Mitchell? Was it Garreth, then? Dex took off running toward the next corner. He stopped and ducked down again, peering around the edge of the wall. The light from a sconce reflected off metal. He swore and lunged back just as a bullet ripped through the corner of the wall, its boom echoing through the tunnel.

Dex raised his gun again and ran past the wall, firing off two quick rounds. The man at the other end dove behind the next corner. Dex took off, running as fast he could. Both his footsteps and the other man's pounded against the hardwood floors. When he reached the next turn, he didn't stop this time. He raced around it, ready to end this.

He turned the corner at full speed. Ah, hell. He raised his arms to protect his face, unable to stop as he slammed against the wall that marked the end of the passage. Stinging pain shot through his shoulder as he busted through a hole in the drywall and slid to the floor. Plaster and dust rained down on him and he waved his hand in front of his face.

Footsteps pounded on the wooden floor again, from the direction where he'd just come from. He raised his gun and aimed it at the corner. He kept his finger on the rail beside the trigger, waiting, waiting.

His nemesis rounded the corner at full tilt. Dex jerked his gun up toward the ceiling just as Amber barreled into his chest. He grunted as he caught the full brunt of her to keep her from crashing into the wall. She let out a little shriek of fear a second before she recognized him.

After quickly stowing the gun, he cradled her against him, his hand shaking as he rubbed it down her back. If he hadn't hesitated long enough to realize she was far too small to be the man he was after, he could have shot her. And, at this close range, he wouldn't have missed.

"Dex, ease up. I can't breathe," she choked.

He forced himself to relax his grip, but he couldn't bring himself to let her go. "Amber, what are you doing in here? I could have killed you," he rasped.

She pushed against his chest and he reluctantly let her go. "I'm sorry. I heard shots. I thought you might be hurt, or need help. I was so scared."

"Scared for me?"

She nodded. "Of course." She ran her hands up and down him as if searching for wounds.

"I'm fine. He didn't hit me. But he got away. I chased him around this corner, but he was gone. There must be another panel here somewhere."

She sat back on her knees. "You saw him?"

"Only in shadow. But I can rule out everyone but Garreth and Mitchell. I'm leaning more toward Garreth now."

"Why?" she asked, as he stood and helped her to her feet.

"Because I called out Mitchell's name and whoever I was chasing laughed."

She shivered. "Creepy."

"Yeah, tell me about it." He felt along the walls. "The panel has to be here somewhere. He couldn't have gotten back down the passageway past me." He ran his hands along the walls, looking for a seam.

Amber stepped farther back toward the corner. "Dex, there, look. I can see some light under the wall over here."

He bent down and studied where she was pointing. "You're right. But I don't see a seam in the wall. It's all drywall."

She shook her head. "I don't think the panel is in the wall. It's in the floor."

He backed up, and, sure enough, there was a darker square of wood in the center of the floor. Once he bent down and studied it, the opening mechanism was immediately clear. A wood knot had been removed and in the depression was a small, round knob no bigger than a quarter.

"You okay covering me?" he asked, holding up the revolver.

She rolled her eyes. "Is a spatterdock yellow?"

"Well, since I have no clue what a spatterdock is, I really couldn't say."

"Of course I'll cover you." She took the gun.

He hesitated. "Be careful. Stand back." He grabbed the little knob, then flung the wooden panel up on its hinge and stood back, expecting the gunman to be hiding below. But no shots rang out. He eased back to the edge and leaned down to get a look inside.

"It's a short tunnel, more or less about ten

feet long. Goes in only one direction. Back toward the way we came. Wait here."

"No way. We're doing this together. No more running off into danger without me. We're a team, Dex."

He didn't like the idea of putting her in danger, but leaving her behind while he continued deeper into the bowels of the house didn't feel safe, either. "All right. But I go first. And before you say it, no, you keep the gun. No arguments on that."

She didn't appear to like his conditions, but she gave him a tight nod.

He braced his hands on both sides of the opening and dropped down into the cramped space, which was only about three feet tall. As soon as he did, the opening above him shut. He glanced up in surprise, noting the ropes and pulleys that had automatically closed the trapdoor and the rubber gasket on this side around the opening, which had stifled any sound.

The door opened again, and Amber looked down at him. "What was that about?"

He motioned toward the pulley system. "Looks like your grandpa designed the door to close on its own so he wouldn't have to close it himself. Assuming he ever ran around in these corridors."

She lowered herself over the opening and

Dex grabbed her around the waist. He gently set her down and the trap door again quietly but quickly closed behind them.

"Cool," she said. "I can't believe he built all of this and never told me. I would have had so much fun as a kid in here."

"Maybe that's why he didn't tell you. He didn't want to worry about you running around in the walls and maybe getting lost or hurt. But why would he even build these tunnels?"

"He was always a bit paranoid. Maybe he thought they'd give him a way to escape if an intruder ever got into the house. Who knows? Do you see another way out?"

He nodded. "This is apparently a short crawl space beneath the floor above, but it's not low enough to be on the first floor or we'd be in water right now. There's another panel on the ceiling, at the end. Probably opens into another passageway. Do you have any idea where we are right now?"

"If I had to guess, from the directions I ran above, we're somewhere near the second-floor library."

They moved to the end of the crawl space and Amber reached up for the panel above them, but Dex pushed her back.

"I go first," he said. "If the killer is waiting for us on the other side, I don't want you to get shot."

"Well, hello, the feeling is mutual. And I'm the one with the gun."

"Doesn't matter. Step back, Amber."

"You're being a Neanderthal. I can protect myself, you know."

He cupped her face in his hands and leaned down to give her a soft kiss. When he pulled back, he searched her eyes. "I know you can protect yourself. You protected *me* back in the swamp. In fact, you saved my life. Now it's my turn, okay? I couldn't forgive myself if something happened to you."

Her eyes turned misty. "You say the sweetest things." She pulled him down for another kiss, and this one wasn't soft. By the time they broke apart, both of them were panting.

Dex was left resenting the killer even more, because if it weren't for him, he'd be back in the bed with Amber right now showing her just how sweet he could be.

He forced himself to step away from her and temptation and studied the panel above him to see how to open it. There, on the top corner, another knot had been removed and there was a knob. At least Grandpa was consistent. Dex reached for the knob.

A muffled scream sounded from above them.

Dex shared a surprised look with Amber, then shoved the knob. The panel flew open, the pulley system helping raise it quickly and silently like the other panel. Dex stood up, noting Amber had been right. This was the library, and the opening was back in a corner surrounded by floor-to-ceiling bookcases. He quickly hopped out and braced the panel to keep it from automatically closing, while Amber followed close behind.

The scream sounded again.

Dex and Amber took off running down an aisle between bookshelves and came out into the end of the library, close to where they'd been sitting earlier that morning.

Aunt Freddie was sitting on one of the couches, her face ghastly pale. Buddy was using a magazine to fan her. Derek stood beside them, and all three stared at Amber and Dex in surprise.

"Where did you two come from?" Derek demanded, his surprise turning to suspicion.

Amber gave Dex a puzzled look as they hurried to the group.

"What's going on?" Dex asked, not bothering with explanations. "Who screamed?"

Aunt Freddie pushed Buddy away and shakily rose to her feet, half leaning on him as he helped her up. "I did." Without another word, she pointed across the room.

Dex and Amber both followed the direction in which she was pointing. There, on top of a side table next to a chair, was a bunched-up white blouse with red splotches on it that looked like blood.

"It's Amy's," Freddie announced. "And she's missing."

Chapter Fourteen

Everyone started talking at once.

Dex held his hands up. "Hold it. Everyone quiet."

The library fell silent. As one, Aunt Freddie, Buddy and Derek looked at Dex. He lowered his hands.

"Okay, I'll start. Amber and I noticed the guns were missing from the trunk earlier, as we were all escaping the floodwaters to go upstairs."

Derek fisted his hands beside him, his jaw tight and angry. "And you didn't think it was a good idea to tell the rest of us?"

"I didn't want to panic anyone. We knew the killer already had a gun somewhere, so it didn't really change things."

"Except to make you the only one with access to a gun." He waved at the Colt that Amber now had tucked into her waistband.

"Or the two of you. Hell, maybe you're both the killers."

Buddy stepped forward, using his bulk to force Derek back a few feet. "No one is going to blame Amber again for another murder, so you can just stop that right now. And as far as that other lady goes, like I already said, Dex and I reached the room at the same time. He couldn't have killed her. Plus, I know who took the guns."

"Who?" Dex and Derek asked at the same time.

"Me. I didn't cotton to the idea of the murderer being the only armed one around here, so I hid them in case we needed them. Looks like that was a good idea after all." He eyed Derek with distaste. "Except I'm not sure who to trust around here."

Derek's eyes narrowed. "Are you accusing me of something, old man?"

"Well, you were the one getting cozy with Amy earlier. And now she's missing."

Derek stepped forward, his hands in fists.

"Stop it, you two." Dex shoved Derek, who glared at him in return. To the others, Dex said, "Derek isn't the threat here."

"And how do you know that?" Aunt Freddie chimed in, standing close to Buddy in a united front against an angry-looking Derek.

"Because someone opened a hidden panel in Amber's room a little while ago. And I'm pretty sure I saw another panel open in Mallory's room earlier and just didn't realize it at the time. The killer is using hidden passageways to get around the house. And I saw him. He's definitely not Derek."

"You saw him?" Derek asked. "Who is it, then?"

"One of the only two men not in this room, Mitchell or Garreth. I only saw him in shadows."

"Then how do you know it's not this guy?" Buddy waved at Derek.

"Because the man I saw was—"

"Taller," Derek said, sounding weary. "I'm the short man out. I get it. Fine. So it's Mitchell or Garreth. One of them has Amy. I say we tear this place apart and find them. After we get those guns."

Buddy shook his head. "Nope. Like I said, I don't trust you. I'll give Freddie a gun, and Dex, though."

"You'll give me one, too." Derek drew himself up as if to intimidate Buddy, but the old man just ignored him. "I'll go get them."

"Wait." Dex held up his hand. "Buddy, Derek arrived in that hallway outside Mallory's room at the same time that we did. And he's not the man who shot at me in the passageways. So I think we can all agree he's not the killer. Derek needs to protect himself, too."

"There are only three guns," Buddy grumbled.

"I've got my knife," Amber said. "And I'll give Dex my gun. You three get the rest of the guns. And we all stay together. We'll all be safe that way."

"She's right. As long as we stay together, we should be safe," Aunt Freddie said. "Give him a gun too, Buddy."

"Oh, fine. Come on. They're over here. I hid them in one of the bookshelves when we brought the food up here." He led them to a shelf at the other end of the room and pulled out the guns. "I don't have any extra ammo, so if we get in a shoot-out, we'll have to be careful."

"Good grief," Dex said. "There's not going to be a shoot-out. If those guns are the types with safeties, keep the safeties on."

"Only a sissy needs a safety." Buddy passed the guns around.

Dex had a very bad feeling about everyone around him being armed, but he couldn't exactly justify being the only one with a gun. "Everyone, please, be careful. I don't want anyone getting shot by accident."

"Son," Buddy said, "the only ones around here who might be careless with firearms are the townies like you and this Dexter feller."

"Derek," Derek corrected.

"Whatever."

Derek shook his head and gave Dex a pained look. For whatever reason, Buddy had taken a dislike to him and wasn't going to drop it.

Dex figured it had to do with the way Derek had been cozying up to Amy earlier. He remembered how the town had been against Jake as an outsider when he'd first come here. But they now considered Jake to be one of their own. They had their hearts in the right places, being protective of one other. But he could well understand Derek's frustration. If it weren't for his own ties to Jake, they'd probably be treating him the same way.

"Okay, when Amber and I got here, we'd just heard you scream, Freddie. So what happened?"

"Something woke me up. I'm not sure what. And I got up and looked over there and saw Amy's blouse, all cut up." She shivered. "Then I went looking for her on the couch on that other side of the room where she and Dexter had been earlier—"

Derek rolled his eyes.

"—and he was lying there asleep but Amy was gone. That's when I screamed."

"So no one saw Amy leave? Or anyone else in here?"

They all shook their heads.

"Maybe she went back to her room," Amber said. "And the killer put that blouse there to scare us?"

"What about the blood?" Derek asked.

She shook her head. "I don't know."

"Let's go to Amy's room and see if she's there before we go down that line of thought," Dex said.

As one they headed toward the door. Dex made them wait while he looked out in the hallway. Clear. Lightning lit up the windows behind them, casting eerie shadows down the hall. But so far the generator was keeping up and the sconces down the hall showed enough that he felt it was safe to step outside.

"Which way?" he whispered to Amber.

"She was in the west wing, a few doors down from… Mallory's room."

He nodded and headed out, with Amber keeping pace with him. The others followed close behind. Dex tried not to think about the fact that they had guns in their hands. His back itched, expecting someone to stumble any minute and shoot him.

"Keep an eye on the doors, and listen for anyone else," he whispered back to them.

Buddy gave him a salute as if Dex was a general, and he whispered to Freddie. She nodded and the two of them aimed their guns at either side as they made their way down the hall behind him. Dex noted that Derek kept his gun shoved into his waistband and stayed well back from Freddie and Buddy, apparently as nervous as Dex was with the two Mystic Glades residents walking around with their guns out.

They passed the open railing that looked down on the foyer below and, as one, they paused. Amber gasped and clutched Dex's arm.

He could well understand her surprise and dismay. Water covered the bottom two steps of the staircase and lapped at the third. "I'm sorry," he said. "I know this is your family home."

She nodded, looking miserable. "I never thought I'd see the day when the water would rise like this. We've had floods in the past, but they never got this high."

"I think the rain's letting up," he said, trying to make her feel better.

She looked out the windows above the front door. "You're right. That's something to be grateful for, at least."

"Come on." He urged her forward, not liking that they were essentially targets out in the open two-story foyer. If Mitchell or Garreth was bold enough to shoot at him, then he wasn't going to assume the man would be worried about getting wet down on the first floor. The attacker could be behind an archway even now, waiting for a good shot.

They passed the open railing and Dex breathed a sigh of relief with walls on both sides again, blocking any shots from below. When they reached Amy's door, Dex didn't bother knocking. If the killer was inside with her, he wanted to use the element of surprise to put the odds more in his favor. He drew his gun, carefully turned the knob, then shoved the door open and ran inside.

Another scream met him as Amy backed up against the wall, clutching a towel against her naked body, her hair dripping water onto the floor.

Dex lowered the gun and shoved it into his waistband. "Are you okay?"

She blinked at him and looked at Amber. "Why does he have a gun? What are all of you doing here?"

Amber hurried to her and gave her a fierce hug before pulling back and answering. "We thought the killer had you."

She frowned. "Why would you think that? I was just taking a shower."

Freddie and Buddy stepped up beside Dex. "One of your shirts was in the library, with blood on it."

Her face turned a light pink. "Oh. Sorry. I scratched my arm against an old nail on one of the bookshelves earlier this morning when I woke up before everyone else. I had a tank top underneath, so I took off my shirt to stop the bleeding. I forgot and didn't take it with me when I left later to take a shower." She frowned. "Where's everyone else?"

Dex shoved his gun into his waistband. "I'm not sure where Garreth and Mitchell are. We think one of them must be the killer. Now that we know that you're okay, our next stop will be to look in Garreth's and Mitchell's rooms to see if either of them is there."

"Okay, but where's Derek?"

Her words seemed to sink into everyone at the same time. They all whirled around.

Derek was gone.

Dex stepped out of Garreth's closet and crossed the bedroom to where Amber was rifling through Garreth's suitcase.

She looked up and shook her head. "I don't know what he brought with him, of course, but everything seems to be in order. No obvious gaps like anything's missing. What about that briefcase he had with him?"

"It's in the closet. I couldn't open it since it's locked. But it's present and accounted for. Unlike Garreth."

"And Mitchell and Derek," she added.

"Told you I shouldn't have given him a gun," Buddy grumbled from his position on the other side of the room next to Amy and Freddie.

"He's not the killer," Dex said. "It has to be Mitchell or Garreth."

"How tall am I?" Buddy asked.

"Excuse me?"

"You heard me, son. How tall am I?"

Dex considered him for a moment. "Five-eight?"

Buddy drew himself up, and Dex immediately realized his mistake. Buddy had been slouching.

"Closer to six foot," Dex admitted.

"Five-eleven," Buddy confirmed. "You willing to bet your life, and ours, that you were right that the man you saw in those hidden passageways wasn't that Dexter fellow?"

"You're right. I shouldn't have made any assumptions. The hallway was dark. And he was far away. I have to allow for the possibility that the killer could be anyone, including *Derek*."

"You mean the killer could be anyone except us." Amber waved her hand to encompass everyone in the bedroom.

"I'm not assuming anything at this point," he said.

Buddy gave him an irritated look. "We're going back to the library."

"Wait." Dex hurried to the door. "The library isn't a safe place to stay. It has one of the passageway entrances. Amber, is there some other room we can all easily fit in, somewhere more defensible?"

She shook her head. "Other than the bedrooms, there are no other big enough rooms upstairs where we could gather."

"Then we need to search the upstairs library to make sure we know where all of the passageway entrances are and block them off. If we have to, we'll scoot furniture on top of any trapdoors or throw a pile of books on them. Before we go back, does anyone need a bathroom break or anything from their rooms? I don't want anyone wandering around on their own."

Amy shook her head no.

Buddy and Freddie both raised their hands like children in a schoolroom.

"Bathroom," Freddie said.

"Me, too," Buddy chimed in.

Dex sighed. "Amber? Where's the nearest bathroom?"

"Just down the hall."

They went through the same routine, Dex looking down the hall and then everyone keeping behind him as they headed out the door. But this time, both Amber and Dex kept looking back to make sure they didn't lose anyone.

Once they were finally in the library and Dex was satisfied that they'd located the only passageway entrance—the one he and Amber had used earlier—and it was covered by a very heavy couch that had been difficult for all of them together to scoot over to the trapdoor, Dex pulled Amber to the side away from the others.

"I need you to stay here and keep an eye on the others, make sure they don't try to go anywhere. Lock the door behind me."

"Hold it." She put her hand on his arm to stop him. "Where do you think you're going? The rain has stopped, yes, but the water won't recede for a while. We need to wait here until we can get back to town and call the police. Even then, we'll likely have to pile into a canoe to get there since the cars are probably all flooded out."

"A canoe? You have one around here?"

She shook her head. "No. I was being facetious. I wish I had a canoe. I could get us out right now, since the lightning has stopped. But I don't."

His excitement at hearing her mention a canoe took a nosedive and cemented his earlier decision. "Okay, let's take a hard look at what we're up against, then. There are three men out there somewhere—two of whom are either already dead or could be soon if I don't find them, and the third is armed and has already killed once for sure and tried to kill me in the passageway. Amber, I can't sit here and wait an entire day for the water to go down while two people are somewhere at the mercy of a killer. I have to search for them."

"Fine. Then I'm going with you."

He grabbed her arm this time. "No. You're not."

"You listen to me, Dex Lassiter. I survived in a dangerous swamp for over two years. Trust me, it's not just the reptiles and wild animals that I had to watch out for. Drug dealers and other unsavory people use those swamps as their personal hiding place and sometimes as a route to ship their illegal cargo. I've had more than a few run-ins with them and I'm still standing here to talk about it. Don't assume that I'm not good in a fight just because I'm a woman. You need someone to watch your back, or you can watch mine. But, regardless, I am going with you."

He gritted his teeth. "How am I supposed to focus when I'm worrying about you out there with me?"

Her face softened and she pressed her hand against the side of his face. "The same way that I will. I care about you, Dex. And I don't want you hurt any more than I think you want me hurt. But I, too, am not going to sit around while your friends need help."

He cupped the back of her neck and pulled her in for a quick kiss. "Damn it, Amber. I don't like you being in danger."

"Neither do I. I'll be careful. We'll both be careful. And we'll get through this together."

He nodded. "All right." He quickly told the others what they were going to do. "Don't let anyone else in this library, no matter what."

"What if Derek comes back?" Amy's concern for him was obvious in the worry lines on her young forehead.

"I suppose you'll have to use your own judgment," Dex said. "But I'd feel a lot better if you kept that door closed until either Amber or I return. We'll search the house in a grid pattern and check in once an hour, which means that our first check-in will be—" he looked at his watch "—three o'clock."

Buddy rose from the couch where he'd been sitting with Freddie. "What are we supposed to do if you aren't back by three?"

Dex took Amber's hand in his and exchanged a long look with her before answering. "Pray."

Chapter Fifteen

Amber held up her thumb, silently letting Dex know that the bathroom connected to the bedroom he was searching was clear. He nodded and headed into the walk-in closet while she waited against the wall by the door, her hand poised on the top of her knife sheathed at her waist. This was the last bedroom to search in the east wing, and they were bumping up against the one-hour mark so they'd have to hurry back to the library for their check-in if they weren't going to worry the others.

She wished they hadn't agreed to the one-hour check-in since it would disrupt their search. But she tried to imagine herself sitting in the locked library, waiting, and realized she'd probably go nuts if hours passed without any word if someone else was out searching. Dex knew what he was doing when he'd told them he'd come back. It was as much for the others' peace of mind as it was for her and Dex's safety. Because she had no doubt that if she and Dex didn't check in, Aunt Freddie would be pushing Buddy to go search the house for them.

Dex emerged from the closet, shaking his head. He met her beside the door and pointed to his watch. She nodded, and they looked out into the hall, then hurried back toward the library, watching every table, every alcove, every door as they passed. She and Dex had made a point of closing and locking each door after they searched a room. So if any of them were open, they'd know that's where someone else had gone.

Their quick trek down the hall was uneventful. Aunt Freddie must have been waiting at the door, because as soon as Amber announced that it was her and Dex, the door swung open.

While Dex spoke to Freddie and Buddy, Amber hurried to Amy, who was staring out the front window at the water below. Amber was just about to speak when she saw Amy's reflection in the glass and hesitated. Instead of the pale, scared-looking young girl that Amber was used to seeing when she looked at Amy, the reflection against the dark windowpane seemed much older, harsh, angry. Her brows were drawn down and her lips were compressed into a tight line.

Amy raised her hand and pressed it against the glass.

Amber's eyes widened and she leaned forward to see what Amy might be looking at.

Amy suddenly turned around, her eyes wide, her face looking frightened like usual as she pressed a hand against her chest. "Amber, my gosh, you scared me."

"I'm sorry. I didn't mean to." She forced a tight smile. Had she only imagined the angry expression on Amy's face reflected in the window? Was it just a trick of the light?

Amy's brows drew down in confusion. "Amber? Is something wrong?" She raised her hand to her throat. "My God. Please tell me you didn't find Derek, and that he's…he's…" She bit her lip and made a small sound in her throat as if she was trying not to cry.

Guilt rose inside Amber and she pulled the other woman into a hug. "I'm so, so sorry. I'm tired and on edge. I should have been more careful and shouldn't have worried you. No, we haven't found Derek." She pulled back and took Amy's hands in hers. "We have to believe that he's okay." *If he isn't the killer.*

"Everything all right over here?" Dex asked from behind her.

Amy's shy gaze darted away. "I'm fine. I

overreacted, thought maybe something had happened to Derek."

Dex smiled. "You really like him, don't you?"

Her face flushed. "He's okay."

"We're doing everything we can to find him. Don't worry."

She bit her bottom lip and wrapped her arms around her waist. "Thank you."

He nodded. "Amber? Ready to search the east wing?"

"The east wing?"

"Yes. The one we haven't searched yet. Ready?"

Something in his gaze told her to go along with what he was saying, even though she knew they'd already searched that wing. "Yes, yes, of course. Let's go."

Dex led her to the door, then stopped and spoke in low tones to Buddy, before pulling Amber out into the hall.

When they were in one of the bedrooms in the west wing a few minutes later, Dex closed the door.

Amber swung around to face him. "Okay, spill. What did you say to Buddy? And why did you lie about where we were going?"

"I told Buddy the truth about us searching the west wing next. But I didn't want Amy to know. I warned Buddy to keep an eye on her, that I didn't trust her. And that if he got a chance to get her gun away from her without openly confronting her, he should take it."

"What? Why?"

"Because if Amy is our enemy, instead of an ally, and she sneaks out of the library to come after us, I don't want her to know where to search. There was something…creepy…about the way she looked at you when you talked to her. For a moment, it almost looked like she… hated you. I hurried over as soon as she turned around."

Amber's eyes widened. "I thought the same thing. Only I noticed her reflection in the window, that she seemed…different, harder, angry. But that doesn't make sense. And why would she hate me? I only just met her."

"I don't know, but since we both got the same vibes, I say we be careful not to turn our backs on her."

"Good grief, is everyone after us now? Do we have to be afraid of all of them?"

"I'd rather be alert and stay alive than take any chances. Come on. Let's get through this wing as fast as we can. I have a feeling we won't be any more successful than we were on the other side."

Sure enough, their search yielded nothing new. No clues. No more passageway doors that they could find or trap doors in the floors. And no sign of Garreth, Mitchell or Derek.

"After the next check-in," Amber said, "I think we should search the only two rooms we haven't been in yet. They're both locked, but the killer may have been able to get inside through the passageways and panels."

"You're talking about your grandfather's bedroom, which has been sealed for years, and my old bedroom—where Mallory was... killed."

She nodded. "I don't like the idea of going in either room. And I know we wanted to keep the crime scene pristine for the police. But we're running out of places to search."

He glanced down the dimly lit hallway toward the closed and locked door where Mallory's body had been found, not looking any more excited about the prospect of going inside than she was.

"How much time do we have?" Amber asked. "We searched faster this time, now that we're in a routine."

He checked his watch. "You're right. We have fifteen more minutes."

"Do you still have the keys?"

He patted his pants pocket. "Okay. Let's do this."

She followed him to his old bedroom door

and they both pressed their ears against the wood, listening for any sounds from within.

Dex very carefully and quietly put the key into the lock and slowly turned it. As soon as the lock clicked, he shoved the door open and ran inside, sweeping his gun out in front of him.

Amber ran in after him, holding her knife out. When she saw what was on the bed, she pressed her hand to her throat. "Oh, no."

Dex was already shoving his gun into his waistband and hurrying to the bed. He bent over Garreth and pressed his fingers against the side of his neck, checking for a pulse.

Amber stopped beside him. "Is he…" She couldn't bring herself to say it. There was blood all over his shirt and his face was incredibly pale.

"No, he's not dead," Dex said. "But his pulse is very weak." He leaned closer. "Garreth, can you hear me? It's Dex."

Garreth moaned, his eyelids fluttering then opening. "Dex?" His voice came out a bare whisper of sound.

"Where are you hurt?" Dex asked, as he opened Garreth's suit jacket. "Oh, no."

"He's been stabbed," Amber said. "Twice, that I can see. We've got to stop the bleeding." She ran into the adjoining bathroom and came back with some towels. Dex was pressing his hands against both wounds. Garreth writhed beneath him, alternately cursing and begging him to stop hurting him.

"I'm sorry," Dex gritted out. "I have to keep the pressure, Garreth."

"I don't think he can hear you." Amber felt his forehead. "He's hot, but I don't know if it's from the blood loss or if he's already got an infection."

"You can help him, though. You helped me."

She gently pushed his hands away and laid the towels on top of Garreth's abdomen, then stepped back for Dex to press down again. Garreth wasn't struggling anymore. He'd passed out from the pain.

"Amber?" Dex's tortured voice called to her. "Please. You have to help him. I don't know what to do, but you do."

She bit her bottom lip. "You don't understand. I don't...do that anymore."

"Amber, you're not responsible for your grandfather's death, if that's what this is about. I know you tried to save him with your tonic, but you couldn't save him. It was the cancer that took his life. You did everything you could. It wasn't your fault."

She clenched her hands at her sides. "I know. Logically, I know that. But in my heart, I can't help wonder if there was something else that I could have done."

He bent down, capturing her gaze. "You can do this. I know you can. What do you need? Tell me. How do we stop the bleeding? How do we bring his fever down? There have to be medicines around here for that, right? A needle? Thread?"

She could do this. She could do this. "Yes, yes, there should be headache powders in my grandfather's bathroom." She swallowed hard at the idea of going in there without Dex. Not because she was scared, but because facing the ghosts of her past would be so much easier with him there to support her. "And I've got needle and thread in my bedroom."

"Take the gun with you. And the keys, so you can get into your grandfather's room." He put his hand on hers. "Be careful. If the crime scene seal from two years ago is broken, don't go in. And even if it isn't, be extremely vigilant." He frowned. "It could be dangerous. I should go. You should stay here."

"No. Stay with your friend. I've got this."

She grabbed his gun and ran before he could stop her.

DEX SWORE, REGRETTING that he'd let her go. But he couldn't do anything about that right now.

He'd just have to hope she was okay, as much as it killed him not to chase after her.

He lifted the towel, cursing again when he saw how much blood had saturated it. He tossed it to the floor and grabbed the second towel that Amber had left with him. One of the wounds seemed to be clotting, but the deeper wound wouldn't quit seeping. And Garreth couldn't afford to lose much more blood.

He looked up at the door. Amber had locked it on her way out. He hadn't meant for her to do that, but he understood why she had—to protect him and Garreth if the killer came back. Everything she did seemed to center around others—keeping them safe, nursing them back to health, protecting them in every way possible. She never put herself first, no matter what. It was the main quality, that and her never-ending courage, that astounded him. He was used to working with people who always put themselves first, who put making a dollar above everything else, including relationships and families. And since almost dying in the plane crash, and then realizing that one of the people he'd trusted every day at his company was also trying to kill him, he'd had to reevaluate his own life and how he treated others.

And he didn't like what he saw.

He'd known Garreth, Derek and Mitchell

for years. And yet, faced with the knowledge that one of them was a killer, he had no real gut feeling for which one it might be. How could he work with them, even double-date with them in the case of Derek, go to football games and supposed team-building events, and never really, truly know them? The longer this debacle went on the more he despised himself and the more he realized that Amber was a better person than he could ever be. She deserved so much more than she had, and he vowed if they survived he would do everything he could to make sure that she never wanted for anything ever again.

Garreth groaned, drawing Dex's attention.

"Dex?" he whispered, sounding groggy. For the first time since they'd gotten there, Garreth's eyes were clear and focused. "What happened?"

Dex laughed with relief. "Hey, man. You tell me. You've got a pair of nasty cuts on your belly."

Garreth winced. "Hurts like hell. Did I get shot?"

"Stabbed. You don't remember?"

He shook his head. "Last I remember we were putting that freezer on top of the island in the kitchen."

Dex frowned. "You must have gotten conked

on the head." He chanced lifting one hand off the towel and felt along the back of his friend's head. "Yeah, you've got a huge goose egg back there, but it's not bleeding. Not anymore at least." He put both hands on the towel and kept up the pressure even though his arms were starting to ache.

Garreth looked around. "Where are we?"

"My bedroom. Or what was my bedroom, until Mallory went in there and…" He shook his head. "This was where we found her earlier. Amber and I searched this wing for you and the others and decided to look in here. Glad we did."

"The others?"

He winced. "Derek and Mitchell are missing. I have to assume one of them killed Mallory. I just don't know which one."

Garreth closed his eyes. "You thought I might be the killer, didn't you?"

"Sadly, yes. I have to admit I don't really know you or Derek or Mitchell like I thought I did. Hell, I don't even know if you have a girlfriend."

A small smile played on Garreth's lips. "Yeah. Her name is Veronica Walker. One of the many women you've dumped on your way to someone else. We're madly in love and plotting our revenge against you for how you treated her."

"Don't make me press harder," Dex joked. "I'm not proud of my past and am only now beginning to realize what a jerk I've been."

Garreth laughed, then groaned. "Damn, that hurts. And I was kidding. No girlfriend. No time. My boss is a real pain in the ass, and the belly, apparently."

"Your pain-in-the-ass boss is going to give you a month off with pay if you promise not to die on him."

"Careful what you promise. I might take you up on that."

"I'm counting on it." He looked toward the door. "Where the hell is Amber?"

"Right here, right here." Her voice sounded from behind him. "You were so busy talking to Garreth that you didn't notice when I came into the room."

"Well, that's a scary thought."

She shrugged. "No harm." She smiled down at the bed. "Nice to see you awake, Mr. Jackson. Let's see about stitching you up and getting that fever down, okay?"

"If it will make this jerk stop pressing on my stomach, I'm up for anything."

Garreth held still like a trouper for Amber to stitch him up, in spite of not having anything more powerful than the headache powder to dull the pain. It was when she and Dex tried to roll him over to check for other injuries that he passed out again.

"What's wrong with him?" Dex asked, worried that they'd hurt him by rolling him over.

Amber finished feeling along his back and motioned for Dex to lay him down before replying. "His belly isn't distended and I don't see any more injuries. I think he's just exhausted and passed out from that and the pain of being moved. I'm certainly no doctor but I don't think he has any internal bleeding. I think your friend's going to be fine."

"You should have let him bleed to death," a familiar masculine voice called out from the doorway.

Dex clawed for his gun.

"Draw on me and I'll shoot both of you."

Dex forced his hand to relax and stared in disbelief at the man he'd trusted and worked with for years. "What's going on, Mitchell?" He positioned himself in front of Amber, hoping to shield her.

"Oh, how sweet. You *are* a couple, aren't you? That was pretty obvious from the get-go. Well, now it's my turn to answer the question you asked our dear friend Garreth there. I do have a girlfriend. Or I *did*, until you *stole* her from me and then cast her aside like garbage, like you do *all* your women." His hand tightened on the pistol he was pointing at Dex. "And her name really was Veronica Walker."

Dex blinked in surprise. "I knew Derek dated Ronnie a while back. But I never knew that you—"

"Shut up. I don't want to hear it."

"But this doesn't make sense. Why are you doing this?"

Mitchell raised the gun higher, squarely pointing it at Dex's chest. "I don't want to hear anything else come out of your mouth except 'yes, sir.' Understood?"

Dex flexed his fingers, dearly wishing he could draw his gun. "Yes, sir," he gritted out.

"Toss the gun on the bed. Oh, and Miss Callahan, toss your knife on the bed, too. Quickly. We don't have much time."

Not seeing a way out without risking getting Amber shot, Dex laid his gun on the bed while Amber discarded her knife.

"Why don't we have much time?" Dex asked.

"Well, because of the floodwaters, of course. The rain may have stopped, but the water's still rising as the runoff from higher ground drains down onto this property. I should know. I've spent a lot of time outside since we got here.

In fact, I'd say I know this property just about as well as Miss Callahan now. Maybe better."

"And why do we care about the rising flood-waters?" Dex pressed.

"Oh, I didn't tell you yet? Because if you don't get to Derek soon, he'll drown, of course. The water will be going over his head. He's tied to the maintenance shed. If you hurry, you just might be able to save him. Of course, the question is, will I shoot you *before* you do, or *after*?" He shrugged. "Who knows?" He stepped away from the door and motioned with his gun. "Get moving."

Derek. How could Dex have ever doubted his friend? And now both Derek and Amber were in danger because of his clouded judgment.

He pulled Amber with him toward the door, keeping himself between her and Mitchell's gun.

Chapter Sixteen

Amber hesitated halfway down the staircase with Dex at her side and Mitchell a few steps behind him. Her toes curled inside her sneakers. Mitchell had been right. The water was still rising even though the rain had stopped and there was no more lightning or thunder. She didn't know how many stairs were underneath the water, but the brackish mess was halfway up the front door. What worried her more than the water was what was under that water. Could a gator have worked its way through one of the windows or the back door?

"Move," Mitchell ordered, from behind her and Dex. "Head to the kitchen and the back porch."

She exchanged a glance with Dex. His brow was furrowed with concern and he gave her a barely perceptible nod, as if to reassure her. She nodded to let him know she was okay. But she really wished she had her knife right now. Or the Colt .45 that they'd been forced to leave back with Garreth. Thank God, she'd finished sewing up his wounds before Mitchell got to them. At least Garreth would have a chance now.

But what about Derek? Was he even still alive? And why was Mitchell doing this? She couldn't imagine that Dex would have treated Veronica so poorly that Mitchell felt bound by some kind of old-fashioned honor code to defend her this way. And even if he did, why had he killed Mallory? She desperately wished she could talk to Dex, that they could try to figure this out together. But she was afraid to do more than breathe after the way Mitchell had pointed his gun at Dex back in the bedroom and ordered him not to say anything.

She held the banister and plopped her foot down to the next stair, splashing into the water. Dex stepped into the water with her, matching her step for step. He was obviously doing everything he could to stay glued to her side, to protect her if he could. But nothing could protect either of them if Mitchell decided to pull the trigger or they stepped on a water moccasin.

Another step, the carpet runner squishing beneath her feet. Another, another. Soon the water was up to her chest, but thankfully her feet were on the floor now. It wouldn't get any deeper. The water was only up to Dex's hips. He reached for her hand and held it tightly as they waded forward.

"Watch out for snakes," she whispered, hoping Mitchell wouldn't hear her and retaliate for her talking. "And gators."

He cursed and watched the water around them with renewed interest.

Mitchell splashed down into the water behind them, not close enough for her or Dex to try to overpower him but not far enough away that he couldn't still shoot them or give them the opportunity to dodge around a corner and hide.

Amber plowed forward through the maze of rooms, through the great room and into the kitchen. She was amazed that the electricity was still on in this part of the house. She'd have expected the water to short-circuit the lights. The kitchen was as bright as ever but looked utterly bizarre with the deep freeze up on the island, water lapping at its base. The familiar hum had her skin crawling at the knowledge that a body was inside that freezer.

Dex squeezed her hand, as if to lend her strength and keep her calm. She glanced up at him as they continued toward the back door where Mitchell had told them to go.

"If there's any way for me to jump him, I will," he whispered. "And you need to run back in and get to Buddy, get the guns and hide somewhere."

"I'm not leaving you," she muttered.

His jaw tightened but he didn't say anything else because Mitchell splashed up behind them.

"Onto the porch," he ordered.

Dex wrestled the door open against the current and stepped out onto the porch. Or what was left of it. Amber couldn't believe the destruction she was seeing as she joined him. They both held on to the posts where the railings were attached, or had been. She moved her foot forward and encountered nothing where she knew a railing should be. Behind the house, trees were down, their branches rising out of the water like ghostly fingers ready to snare an unsuspecting person in their grasp.

"Dex," a voice called out. "Dex!"

Amber followed Dex's gaze. As Mitchell had said, Derek was tied to the post that supported the overhang of the maintenance building fifty yards away. His hands were above his head, roped to the post. And he was struggling to keep his chin above the waves the current made as it lapped against the building.

"Go ahead," Mitchell said. "Go help your

friend. Unless you want to save your own hide, like always. That's what I'd expect you to do, of course—stay here and watch out for your own safety rather than brave that murky water. Because that's what you do, put yourself before others."

Dex took a step toward Mitchell.

Mitchell raised the gun toward his head. "Give me a reason, boss. I've been wanting to do this for a long time."

"Really? How long? Before or after you sabotaged my plane?"

Mitchell laughed, the same eerie laugh Dex had heard in the passageway outside Amber's bedroom earlier tonight. Maybe if he'd paid more attention to his employees, to the people in his life, he'd have recognized that laugh. And he'd have known earlier who the killer was. Of course, Mitchell had already disappeared by then, so it wouldn't have mattered. But what did matter right now was saving Amber and Derek and the others inside. He just wished he knew how he was going to manage all that.

"Mitchell, you're not a bad person. I know something must have happened to make you snap. A jury would understand that, too. Stop this, before it goes too far."

Mitchell sneered at him. "Too far? I've already killed Mallory. I'd say I've already gone too far. I didn't mean to kill her, you know. She caught me sneaking into your room with a gun. It was you that I wanted to kill. I shot her without thinking about it."

Dex edged closer to Mitchell. Amber looked toward the maintenance building. Derek's cries were getting weaker. She didn't know how much longer he could keep his chin above the water.

"You panicked then," Dex said, his voice soothing as he spoke to his assistant. "People will understand that. Like you said, you didn't mean to kill—"

"Stop it," Mitchell shouted. He wrapped both hands around his pistol and shook it at Dex. "Just stop it. You and your smooth talking. Do you think I'm stupid?"

Dex held his hands up placatingly. "Of course not. I think you're very smart. You've been practically running my company for years. You do a far better job than I ever could."

"Damn straight, I do." Mitchell lowered the gun ever so slightly. "And what do I get for it? I get to watch you, year after year, treat people like they're nothing."

"Mitchell—"

"Let me finish! You do, you know. You act

all nice and polite on the surface, but do you really care about anyone? No. We're all replaceable, interchangeable. Me. Ronnie. Mallory. I liked Mallory, you know, even though she didn't like me back. Ronnie does, though. She loves me. Because after you threw her away, after you broke her, she came back to me again. You didn't know that, did you? I was there to help her pick up the pieces, to make her realize she had worth. To let her know she mattered and shouldn't have been thrown away like that. You don't give a damn about anyone, Dex. I thought killing you with the plane crash would be quick and painless and would end it all without anyone else getting hurt. I was being merciful. But, of course, you had to survive—the golden boy. Well, now I'm teaching you a lesson before you die. Because for the first time ever, I've figured out what you really care about."

"Mitchell, look, I'm—"

"Don't you even want to know what it is?" he shouted.

"Of course, of course. What do I care about?"

Mitchell swore. "Even now, you don't know. Because you're shallow, empty. Move, get over there."

"No."

Amber stiffened behind Dex. She wanted to see Mitchell's reaction, but Dex kept adjusting his position every time she tried to look around him. He was keeping himself firmly between the two of them.

"Dex?" Derek cried weakly across the darkness.

"Give me the gun, Mitchell," Dex said. "No one else has to get hurt. Let me help Derek and then we'll sit down and talk about what I've done to wrong you. I'll make it right. I promise."

A guttural, pained sound like that from a wounded animal came from Mitchell. Water swished. Amber looked back at the wall of windows in the kitchen. She could see his reflection now. He'd waded through the water and was standing directly in front of Dex, with his pistol jammed against Dex's forehead.

"Don't tell me what to do ever again," Mitchell spit out. "Now, go save Derek like a good boy. And the one thing you care about, the one *person* you care about, will stay here. With me." He suddenly reached around Dex for Amber.

Dex grabbed Mitchell's arm and shoved the gun up toward the ceiling. "Run, Amber! Run!"

The two men struggled for the gun. It went

off, firing into the porch ceiling. They fell backward, a tangle of arms, with Mitchell snarling and cursing at Dex as they both struggled for control of the pistol. They fell into the water and disappeared below the surface.

Amber took a deep breath and crouched down under the water, but when she opened her eyes she couldn't see anything and the burn and sting of the dirty water had her squeezing her eyes shut again. She felt the water move violently around her and she hurriedly stood up above the surface again, wiping at her eyes as she tried to see what was happening.

Dex and Mitchell were standing up again, pressed against the back of the house, still fighting for the gun. Dex managed to free one arm and swung his fist toward Mitchell's jaw. Mitchell jerked to the side before it could connect.

"Amber, get the hell out of here," Dex yelled at her, meeting her gaze in the reflection in the windows.

She realized several things at once. There was nothing she could do to help Dex in his deadly struggle with Mitchell without getting in the way. She was distracting him by staying here. But there was one thing she could do to help. She could save Derek.

She moved toward the edge of the porch.

"Amber, no, it's too dangerous!" Dex cried, confirming her fear that she was distracting him.

"Don't worry about me," she yelled back. "I've got this." She jumped into the water.

DEX LET OUT a guttural roar and crashed his fist into the side of Mitchell's face. Mitchell grunted in pain but didn't let go of the pistol. Dex twisted violently, renewing his struggles in a frenzy, but it took all his strength to keep from getting swept away in the current and still keep Mitchell from lowering the gun and aiming it toward Amber.

Dear God, Amber. He couldn't believe she'd jumped into the water. He had to help her.

"I'm sorry for whatever you think I did to you," he yelled. "Killing Amber or anyone else isn't going to make up for it, though."

Mitchell snarled and kicked toward him, but the force of the water slowed his movements and Dex was able to turn his thigh to block him. Still, the blow knocked him back enough so that Mitchell was able to tug his non-gun hand loose from Dex's hold and put both hands on the pistol. Slowly and surely he began to turn the pistol down toward Dex's head.

Dex swore and shoved Mitchell harder against the house. The mad light in Mitchell's eyes told him there was no reasoning with him. And, damn, the man was stronger than he looked. Dex grabbed the pistol with both hands and lifted his feet. He crashed back against the water's surface, pulling Mitchell down with him under the water.

Chapter Seventeen

Amber struggled to untie the ropes that held Derek to the post. Her hands kept slipping in the brackish water. "Hold on, Derek. Just hold on."

His mouth went under water and again Amber grabbed him and yanked him higher. He coughed out some brackish water and drew a shaky breath. His arms were shaking from the effort of trying to keep his elbows bent to hold himself above the water, but it was a losing battle. He was exhausted.

"If I can just get this knot free." She pulled and plucked at the knot. Derek didn't respond and she didn't expect him to. His eyes were closed. He was using every ounce of strength he had just trying not to drown. He must have been struggling out here for hours and there was nothing left. He seemed ready to pass out from exhaustion. And from the bruises already beginning to form near his temple, she suspected that Mitchell might have hit him. A head injury and exhaustion could be a lethal combination right now. She looked past him to the porch and froze. Where were Mitchell and Dex?

Derek went under again.

Amber grabbed his chin and pulled him up. "Come on, cough it out."

Derek's head lolled back toward the water.

"Derek, Derek, wake up. Cough out the water." She let go of the post and cupped his face with both hands. The current tried to drag her away from the building. She was forced to grab the post again and wrapped her legs around it before reaching for Derek, who'd dropped his face back beneath the water.

"Come on," she yelled. She slapped his cheeks, again and again.

He flinched and opened his eyes. Then he started violently coughing. Water and vomit rolled out of his mouth.

Amber tilted his head so he wouldn't choke. "There you go, that's it. We'll get you out of here. You just have to hang on a little longer."

Water splashed beside her. She gasped and whirled around. A dark shadow rose from below the surface. Gator! No! She grabbed Derek and kicked out with her feet, hitting the reptile under the water.

It broke the surface, coughing and spitting water. Amber's jaw dropped open. This was no gator.

"Dex? Dex! How did you get here? Are you okay?"

He grabbed the post beside her and rubbed his chest. "You have a mean kick. I'm not sure you needed my help, after all." Impossibly, he grinned. And winked.

She sputtered. "I can't believe you're smiling at a time like this."

His smile faded. "Me, either." He looked back to the house. "I don't know where Mitchell went. I knocked the gun loose but he disappeared beneath the water. He could be anywhere." He looked at Derek and the ropes holding him to the post. "Hold on. I'll be right back."

"Dex, don't leave me, don't..."

He disappeared beneath the surface again. Where had he gone? What was he doing? She focused on keeping Derek's chin above the water, cradling his head against her chest as she kept an eye on their surroundings. She didn't know if she was more worried about gators or Mitchell. Both were deadly.

Metal creaked behind her somewhere. She jerked around. "Dex?" Nothing.

Derek coughed up more brackish water.

"It's okay," she soothed, keeping his chin up. "It's okay. Dex wouldn't really leave us. He'll come back."

"Damn straight."

She whirled around. "Dex!"

He smiled again and pulled a machete up from beneath the water. "I remembered this from before, from inside the building." He pulled himself to the backside of the post and held the machete with both hands as he hacked down against the wood. The ropes split and fell away.

Derek slipped from Amber's hands into the water. "No, no!"

Dex dove under and came up seconds later with his friend, holding his head up. "Come on, Amber. Let's get him back to the house and get out of this swamp."

"You don't have to tell me twice."

They swam on both sides of Derek, wrestling against the current and to keep him from going under. He'd completely lost consciousness now and was deadweight, threatening to drag them away or under. Something splashed not far from them.

"Keep swimming," Dex yelled. "Hurry."

His urgency had her putting everything she had into her strokes as she kicked her legs behind her. They reached the porch and she grabbed the post to pull herself up. Dex gave her and Derek a mighty shove forward, which propelled them all the way to the kitchen doorway. She wrestled Derek inside and propped his arms up on a countertop to keep his head above the water.

She turned back to see where Dex was and saw him raise the machete above his head at the edge of the porch and bring it slashing down. An enormous gator snapped its jaws inches from his face, then disappeared beneath the water.

"Dex!" Amber screamed.

He dropped the machete and dove toward the doorway. He pulled himself inside and shoved the door closed. A loud thump shook the door but it held. The gator must have given up because it didn't try again. Dex turned around, his face pale and his eyes wide. "Tell me that did not just happen."

Amber's hands shook as Dex rose to stand in the hip-deep water and helped her hold on to Derek.

"I can't believe you just fought an alligator," she said, her voice hoarse. "And that was a big gator."

He grinned. "Something to brag about later." His smile faded and he glanced around. "If we survive this, that is. I'm not going to assume that Mitchell drowned. We need to get out of here. We're too exposed." He pressed his hand against Derek's chest, then felt the side of his neck. "He's breathing, and his pulse is good. Let's get him upstairs with the others."

"How will we—"

In answer, he lifted Derek and draped him over his shoulder in a fireman's hold. "Let's go. Hurry."

They waded through the kitchen to the great room. Some of the furniture was floating and they had to maneuver around it.

A guttural roar and a splash sounded behind them. They whirled around. Mitchell pointed his gun toward Dex. He dove out of the way. Shots boomed. The front windows exploded in a hail of glass.

Amber grabbed Derek, who was floating facedown, and turned him faceup in the water. Mitchell whirled around, not seeming to notice her. He was too busy looking for Dex. She took advantage of his preoccupation and floated Derek to one of the chairs that was bobbing in the water. She wrestled Derek's arms and upper body into the chair and made sure his face was well above the waterline before she let go.

Mitchell turned toward her, as if just realizing she might be a threat. She dove down below the water. A concussion of movement burst just past her head in the water as a bullet shot at her. She couldn't see, but she swam toward where she remembered the nearest wall to be. When she reached the wall, she used her arms and legs to kick the water to stay below the surface until her lungs were burning. Unable to stay there any longer, she stood up and drew a deep breath as she looked around for Dex or Mitchell.

Mitchell stood ten feet away, his back to her. But he must have heard her as she'd broken the surface. He whirled toward her, gun in hand. Water splashed on his other side as Dex rose above the water with something in his hand. The poker from the fireplace! He brought it crashing down as Mitchell brought his gun around. The gun went off as the poker slammed into the side of Mitchell's head. He cried out and fell back into the water. He raised the gun again, but Dex brought the poker down and knocked it out of his hands. Mitchell sank below the surface.

Dex held the poker at the ready, watching the water all around him. When Mitchell didn't reappear, Dex swore and dropped the poker. He disappeared beneath the water.

Amber pushed off the wall to help him. She'd just reached where she'd last seen Dex when he stood up, pulling Mitchell with him. Mitchell's head lolled against his chest, blood running from the nasty gash in his scalp where the poker had hit him. His eyes were closed.

"Is he…is he dead?"

Dex pressed his hand against Mitchell's neck. "No." He swallowed hard, his Adam's apple bobbing in his throat. "But I hit him hard, too damn hard."

Amber was shocked at the anguish in Dex's voice. "Dex, you did what you had to do. You saved us."

He nodded, but she didn't think he was necessarily agreeing with her. "Derek?"

She pointed to the chair. "He's okay."

He nodded again and started pulling Mitchell toward another chair floating beside that one. He'd just propped Mitchell up when bright lights shone through the hole where the front windows had been shattered.

"Get behind me," Dex ordered. He reached for her just as the front door burst open. Then he grinned and let out a relieved laugh as a man whom Amber had never seen before led a rescue crew of a half dozen Collier County firemen into the house.

"If you're here to save us," Dex said, "you're a little late."

The man in front of the others splashed toward them. His brow was lined with worry as he took in the scene, looking from Derek to Mitchell, then to Amber and Dex.

"I thought we were rescuing you from what I'm told is the worst flood this place has seen in decades. But you managed to up the ante to a whole new level. What the hell happened?"

"It's a long story. I'll explain it all, but first we need medical help for these two."

As the firemen tended Mitchell and Derek, Dex led Amber through the water to the stairs with the man he'd just spoken to following behind.

"There are more people upstairs." Dex helped Amber out of the water and onto the first dry step.

"Aren't you going to introduce us?" Amber nodded to the man beside Dex.

"Oh, sorry. Amber Callahan, this is—or was, until he quit—the other half of Lassiter and Young Private Investigations. Meet Jake Young."

AMBER PAUSED IN the doorway to Derek's room in Naples Community Hospital, with two paper coffee cups in her hand. Derek was asleep, resting comfortably in spite of the IV he'd vehemently opposed when he'd first gotten there. Apparently he was afraid of needles, but Amy had shamed him into "taking it like a man," and had added the extra insult that Garreth was being much less of a baby in his room down the hall, even though Garreth's injuries had been more severe.

Chagrined, Derek had allowed the nurse to put the IV in his arm. They were giving him antibiotics through that IV to counteract any bacteria he may have swallowed when he'd nearly drowned in the swamp. And they were monitoring him because of the concussion he'd suffered. But he'd probably be released in a few days as long as he didn't show signs of a fever.

Amy was asleep, too, sitting in a chair pulled up beside the bed, her upper body and arms draped across Derek's chest. Their hands, even in sleep, were laced together. Amber had a feeling this wasn't a mild infatuation that was going to blow over. The two of them seemed completely enamored with each other. The anger that Amber had thought she'd seen in Amy's reflection in the library window? She realized now it was probably a mixture of anger and pain because she was worried—and mad—that someone might have hurt Derek.

Amber backed out of the room, allowing the door to quietly close behind her as she turned and balanced the coffee cups.

"Is one of those for me?"

She looked up sharply, expecting to see Dex. But instead, it was his friend, Jake.

"You don't have to look so disappointed." He shoved away from the wall.

"Oh, sorry. I wasn't…I thought…" She held out one of the coffee cups. "If you like cream and sugar, it's yours. I was bringing it to Amy, but she's asleep."

He grimaced but took the cup anyway. "I prefer black, but right now I'll take anything warm after being submerged in that nasty swamp. Thanks." He took a deep sip and grimaced again. "Or not." He tossed the cup in a nearby trash can.

Amber eyed her own cup. "That bad, huh?"

"I wouldn't try it if I were you."

She tossed it in the trash. "Thanks for saving me. Again."

He shook his head. "I didn't save you. Dex gets all the credit for that. Speaking of which, he's asking about you."

She cleared her throat. "He is?"

"Uh-huh. He wanted me to come get you. He's sitting with Mitchell. I couldn't get him to leave the guy's side."

"Mitchell? Why would Dex sit with him after everything that happened?"

"You can ask him that yourself. Come on.

I'll take you to him." He offered his arm like an old-fashioned gentleman. Amber smiled and took it and walked with him down the long hall to another wing of the hospital. He stopped at room 222.

"I'll be in the waiting room, just around the corner when you come out," he said. "Faye just got to the parking lot. She's coming up. She'd love to see you."

"And I'd love to see her."

He nodded and headed to the waiting room.

Amber could see why Dex liked Jake. He was a nice guy. And he and Faye had cut their Bahamas honeymoon short to check on Dex, after hearing about the terrible storm and that the plane crash had been deliberate. They'd been keeping tabs on him through Freddie until Freddie told them they were heading to the old mansion to celebrate Amber's charges being dropped.

After that, when the impending storm was on the news, Faye had had a premonition that it was going to get worse than the weathermen thought. She'd convinced Jake they should fly back from the Bahamas before the weather prevented them from doing so, and check on Dex and the others.

But the storm had come in even faster than Faye's premonition had told her. And it had taken a long time to work their way to Mystic Glades. By that time, they knew anyone in the mansion might be in trouble, so Jake had rounded up some firemen and some canoes and they'd made their way through the flood.

"You coming in or planning on standing in the hallway all day?"

She whirled around at the sound of Dex's voice. He was standing in front of her, outside Mitchell's door. Amber raised a shaky hand to her chest. "You and Jake are both good at that."

"Good at what?"

"Surprising people." She waved her hand. "Never mind. Jake said you wanted to speak with me."

He pushed open the door behind him. "Do you mind talking inside?"

She hesitated. "In Mitchell's room?"

"He's in a medically induced coma, to keep the brain swelling down. He won't hear anything we say."

She rubbed her hands up and down her arms, not at all anxious to go near Mitchell again. "I've heard of studies that say that people in comas *do* hear what is said around them."

"Amber. Please."

His quiet, resolved tone had all kinds of alarm bells going off in her head, but she pushed back her reservations and followed him into Mitchell's room. She stopped just inside, surprised to feel a tug of empathy when she saw the machines and tubes hooked up to the man who'd tried to kill her and Dex a handful of hours earlier.

"He can't hurt you now." Dex waved toward one of two plastic-and-metal chairs beside the window.

She crossed the room and sat beside him. "Why are you here? With him? After everything he did?"

"That's what I wanted to talk to you about."

He scrubbed the stubble on his face. His exhaustion was broadcast by the tiny lines around the corners of his eyes and the dark circles beneath them.

He took her hands in his. "The doctors performed a CT scan. But it wasn't where I hit Mitchell with the poker that they're worried about. What they're concerned with is the mass they found, something called anaplastic astrocytoma. I'm sure I'm pronouncing it wrong, but basically he has a malignant brain tumor."

She blinked in surprise. "A brain tumor?"

"They'll do surgery, radiation, maybe chemo, too. His prognosis doesn't look good. But they'll do everything they can to control the pain and alleviate his symptoms." He tugged his hands out of hers. "He must have been having terrible headaches the past few months. I never even noticed. I was oblivious. How many times did I say good morning without really talking to him, to see how he was really doing?"

"Wait. Dex, is this why you're sitting here with him? You feel guilty?"

He shrugged. "I am guilty—guilty of not paying enough attention. Guilty of being so self-absorbed that I didn't notice that an employee, a friend who's worked for me for years, was acting differently, that he was in pain. I'm guilty of everything he accused me of when we were fighting on that porch." His bleary gaze captured hers. "I'm sorry, Amber. That's what I wanted to tell you. I'm so sorry if I ever treated you that way. And I'm sorry that I took advantage of you. I made an unforgiveable mistake. I shouldn't have—"

"Stop it. Stop it right now. You did not take advantage of me. And I refuse to sit here while you characterize our sleeping together as a mistake. Dex, I wanted to make love with you. I still want to make love with you. Nothing Mitchell said has changed that, or how I feel about you. I want to be with you. Don't you want to be with me?"

His brow furrowed and he looked away. "Of course I want to be with you. But I can't. It's not right."

"How is it not right?" When he didn't answer, she followed the direction of his gaze. He was watching the readouts on the machines by Mitchell's bed. "The tumor affected Mitchell's judgment, didn't it? I'm sure the doctors must have said something like that. Mitchell skewed everything in his mind because he couldn't help it, he couldn't control what the tumor was doing to his brain, to his thoughts."

She waited, but when he didn't say anything, she tried another approach. "Okay, Mitchell has an out, then. There's an explanation for why he did what he did. It will be hard to forgive him, but I'll try because I understand it wasn't entirely his fault. But I can't forgive you."

He jerked his head toward her, his eyes wide. "What?"

"You heard me. If you choose to go down this path of self-loathing and give up the one good thing sitting in front of you, don't expect me to participate in your pity party. I deserve better. *You* taught me that."

"Wait, I taught you that? What do you mean?"

She sighed. "Dex, I gave up two years of

my life because of guilt. Oh, I was pretty sure that I hadn't killed my grandfather with that tonic. I figured there had to be another explanation, and even after I heard about the peanut oil, I wasn't totally convinced that was the cause of his death. But I chose to run, not just to draw suspicion away from Buddy, to protect him if he'd made a horrible mistake. I ran because I knew that living in that swamp would be incredibly difficult, maybe even impossible, but I didn't believe that I deserved any better. I thought I deserved to struggle every day because of the horrible mistake that I'd made."

He frowned. "What mistake? Your grandfather died of cancer. Even if you didn't know it back then, you said you didn't think your tonic killed him."

"No, I didn't. But it didn't save him, either. I was…arrogant. I healed people even when Aunt Freddie's Doc Holliday couldn't heal them. My herbs and potions had never failed me before, and I believed I could do better for Grandpa than real doctors." She shook her head. "My arrogance is what killed my grandfather. I should have insisted that he go to the hospital instead of just assuming that I could take care of him. Would it have made a difference? Probably. But not for long. All it would have done is buy him a few more weeks, weeks filled with pain because of the cancer. I know that now. And because of your faith in me, in getting me to help Garreth and making me fight for others, I realized I was guilty of what you're doing now—of feeling sorry for myself while life passed me by."

She clasped her hands in her lap. "Dex, I wasted two years of my life over guilt when I should have been making up for my wrongs by helping others. The guilt that ate me up is something I have to move beyond if I'm going to make up for my past mistakes. And that's what you have to do. You have to let the guilt go, move on."

She waved at Mitchell, lying in the bed. "You're not responsible for Mitchell killing Mallory. But if you believe he was right when he talked about you using others, about not paying attention to those around you and being self-absorbed, then do something about it. You can start by admitting the truth—that you care about me."

He stared at her as if in shock. "You heard what he said, about Ronnie, about how I treated her. She and Mallory were only a couple of the women I've treated badly over the years. How could you even want me after knowing that?"

She thumped his chest. "It's precisely because you're sitting here acknowledging your past mistakes that I want you. You're a good man." She flattened her hand over his heart. "You're a good man, here. Where it counts. That's the man I'm falling in love with. Because he cares about his impact on other people, and he wants to make it right."

He suddenly scooped her onto his lap. He hugged her so tightly she could barely breathe, but she didn't push him away. Instead, she wrapped her arms around his neck and held on tight, pressing her head against his chest, listening to the solid beat of his wonderful, caring, loving heart.

He kissed the top of her head and loosened his hold, pulling back to meet her gaze. "I don't deserve your faith and trust, or your…love… Amber Callahan. But I'll spend the rest of my life trying to earn it. That is, if that's what you want."

She blinked back the moisture suddenly blurring her vision. "The rest of your life? That's quite a commitment from a commitment-phobe when you barely know me."

He framed her face in his hands. "I know

you. I know the kindness inside you, the way
you put others first. I know that you're one of
the few people who's ever stood up to me, told
me I'm not perfect, that I'm wrong. I've surrounded myself by yes-men and yes-women,
afraid to tell me the truth. I need you to keep
me honest, to tell me when I'm being an ass,
to remind me to stop, and listen, and pay attention—to make me a better person. You're
everything I need and want in my life. If you'll
have me."

Her lips trembled and she drew a shaky
breath. "If that's a proposal, you'd better be
sure about it. Because I just might take you
up on it."

"Is that a yes?"

"It's a qualified yes."

He frowned. "Qualified?"

"I'll only say yes if you agree to take me
away from Mystic Glades. I don't ever want to
go back there again." She shivered with genuine abhorrence at the thought of returning to
the swamp she used to love but that had become the symbol of all her failings.

He cocked his head, looking deep in
thought. "I don't know. It might be hard giving
up being a cop. Especially if I can convince

Deputy Holder to give me a gold star to wear on my chest."

She arched a brow. "So you like the swamp, the alligators, the water moccasins?"

A sexy grin curved his mouth, taking her breath away. "I like *you*, Amber Callahan. And if I have you, with me, forever, I can give all of that up."

"Even the gold star?" she teased.

His grin faded and his gaze searched hers. "I would give up anything, everything, for you. I love you, Amber. Marry me?"

She smiled through the tears freely coursing down her cheeks now. Had she thought she was falling in love with this man? She'd been wrong. She'd already fallen. She was madly, deeply, in love with him. And she couldn't imagine her life without this amazing, caring man in it.

"I love you, too, Dex Lassiter. And the answer is yes."

He kissed her, and for the first time in years, she felt protected, cherished, loved. From the beginning, when she'd spent those summers with her grandfather as an escape from her parents, and later when she'd fled to the Glades, she realized she'd been running *to* something as much as away *from* something. She'd been searching for that one thing her whole life—a home. And she'd finally found it, the place where she belonged. She'd found her home at last, in Dex's arms.

* * * * *

Look for more books in Lena Diaz's
MARSHLAND JUSTICE
miniseries later this year!